## "I won't be your mistress!"

Slade seemed unperturbed by her outburst. "Don't you think you should think it over?"

He didn't want to understand, Lee realized. If only this man didn't hold so much magnetism for her. He knew she couldn't resist him when he got this close.

"We could have a wonderful time." The confidence in Slade's voice increased as he watched her hesitate. "How about a few weeks in the Caribbean?"

"I won't be bought, I tell you!" Lee blinked incredulously. "If you believe I'm not good enough to marry your cousin, why should you even want to contaminate yourself by having another affair with me?"

Slade's face hardened. "I hope this doesn't mean you intend carrying on with the engagement."

Lee wished she could say it did....

# Books by Margaret Pargeter

These books may be available at your local bookseller.

Don't miss any of our special offers. Write to us at the following address for information on our newest releases.

Harlequin Reader Service
P.O. Box 52040, Phoenix, AZ 85072-2040
Canadian address: P.O. Box 2800, Postal Station A,
5170 Yonge St., Willowdale, Ont. M2N 6J3

# MARGARET PARGETER

## impasse

**Harlequin Books**

TORONTO • NEW YORK • LONDON
AMSTERDAM • PARIS • SYDNEY • HAMBURG
STOCKHOLM • ATHENS • TOKYO • MILAN

Harlequin Presents first edition December 1985
ISBN 0-373-10845-1

Original hardcover edition published in 1985
by Mills & Boon Limited

# CHAPTER ONE

LEE MOREAU clenched her hands in an effort to stop them from trembling. She wasn't particularly proud of her past, but she had had reason to hope, during the last few years, that it wouldn't catch up with her. In returning to the Thames Valley, she had known the risk she was taking, but after not hearing a thing from Slade Western for over five years, she had began to feel safe.

Safe enough to get engaged to a man distantly related to him, who used to do a lot of legal work for him. Now, if her instincts served her right, the arrogant dark head in the car that had just shot past belonged to Slade and none other. She prayed she was wrong, because if it had been Slade all her plans for a quiet and contented future might come to nothing. When she was nineteen she had agreed to live with him for two years, but had left him after only six months. She hadn't seen him since and had no idea whether he had looked for her or not, or if he had known where she was. Surely, if he had come back after all this time, it couldn't be because he was seeking her out to collect the debt of time she owed him, or to prevent her from marrying one of his relations. The insatiable desire, or was it hatred, he had once felt for her, must surely have died by now.

With numb fingers Lee packed her sketch pad away in her rucksack and slung it over her back before wheeling her motor-cycle from behind the clump of bushes out on to the road. After carefully adjusting her helmet over the thickness of her luxuriant red hair, she used the kick-starter roughly and when the engine roared into life, raced off as though the devil himself was pursuing her. She took corners too fast and dangerously, but she was suddenly desperate to get home. She tried to tell herself it was ridiculous not to feel safe any more. She had to be mistaken about Slade, she just had to! Without realising she was repeating this over and over again, she turned off the narrow country road on which she was travelling and sped down the bumpy drive to River Bend.

It was nearly seven. She had intended getting back sooner. She must have stayed concealed in the woodland thicket, reduced to a state of shock, for longer than she'd thought. She only wished in her heart she could believe it when her common sense suggested she had been having hallucinations. The strange telepathy which had existed between Slade and herself couldn't possibly be working after all these years. It was because she had been jumpy ever since her engagement had been announced that she imagined every dark-haired man driving a fast car must be Slade. Even had he learned of her week-old engagement there was nothing he could do about it. He had no hold over her apart from a broken promise, a promise which had only been extracted in the first place by means of blackmail.

Parking her bike in one of the garages, beside her small car, Lee stared at it blindly for a few moments before hurrying into the house. River Bend was really an old roadhouse which her grandfather had run as a restaurant. Since he died, Lee had continued to live there, as he had begged her to, but the restaurant had been closed even before this and she had never reopened it. Instead, she endeavoured to make a living from writing and illustrating children's books and filling the empty rooms with a few people whom she liked and trusted, who wanted somewhere quiet to live.

The three people who occupied Lee's spare rooms now had been with her for almost four years. One was the girl who had helped her to take care of her grandfather during his last illness. Julia Brown had changed from hospital to private nursing, but wherever she was working, she and another nurse, Sandra Peel, who was her friend, preferred living here, rather than in more soulless digs in town. Lee's third guest, Nigel Blakey, was an electronics expert employed in the Western works in Reading. He was in love with Julia and Lee admired his dogged perseverance, for Julia seldom seemed aware of his existence. Sandra was more of an enigma. Lee suspected she was in love with someone, but she had become so withdrawn lately it was almost impossible to talk to her.

It was Sandra whom Lee found in the kitchen, this evening, as she crossed the hall and hurried into it. She and her three boarders had a rather unusual arrangement that worked. Instead of her charging them so much a week, they shared all the bills and chores with her. She hadn't wanted to make money out of her friends, it was their company she valued more than anything. She could make enough from writing to live on, but River Bend, surrounded as it was by lonely fields and woods, was curiously isolated, especially in winter.

Tonight it was Sandra's turn to cook dinner, and Lee sniffed appreciatively after apologising for being late. 'Something smells good!' she smiled.

Sandra returned her smile rather stiffly. 'Hello there,' she replied. 'Did you have a good day?'

'Yes—and no,' Lee answered absently. 'And you?'

'So-so,' Sandra shrugged.

For once, Lee was too absorbed with something else to notice Sandra's cool withdrawal. Still thinking of Slade, she asked without meaning to, 'Has anyone called or rung?'

Sandra obviously thought Lee was thinking of her fiancé. 'Matt's coming to dinner, isn't he?' she remarked curtly. 'Why should he ring?'

Because Sandra seemed puzzled by the apprehension she had failed to hide, Lee forced her taut muscles to relax and invented a hasty excuse. 'He's been so busy lately, I had a feeling he wouldn't turn up.'

'Well, there's been nothing since I got in,' Sandra muttered morosely, 'and if you don't hurry, he'll be here before you've had time to change.'

Lee nodded, yet hesitated a moment, wishing she could find the courage to ask what was wrong. Then, sighing helplessly, she continued on her way to her bedroom. Here she forgot about Sandra as she closed the door sharply and flung herself across her bed. The violent movement might have provided some release for her over-slender body, but none at all for her tortured mind. At last, fearing her head was about to burst, she turned on her back and lay staring at the ceiling, twisting her engagement ring nervously.

She had tried to tell Matt about Slade, but he would never listen. Perhaps if she had mentioned Slade by name he might have, but she had never been able to bring herself to go as far as that. Looking back, she saw that her relationship with Slade had been so discreet that none but a few of Slade's most intimate friends, overseas, had ever known they were living together. Yet it was odd that Matt had never guessed, for in that distant summer when, at eighteen, she had first come to live here, Slade had made no secret of his wish to possess her. He had frightened Lee in those days, with his proprietorial attitude, the way he had had of staring at her with eyes often savagely dark whenever he caught her looking at another man. But while she had feared him, she had been drawn to his way of life like a moth to a flame. And, like a moth, she had eventually got her wings singed.

Matt, bless him, appeared to believe it impossible for any girl to reach the age of twenty-four and still be innocent.

'I don't want to hear about your past, darling,' he had stopped her so often she had given up. 'I'm not inexperienced myself, and I've no wish to feel forced to reciprocate your confidences.'

Dear Matt, he must be worth a dozen Slade

Westerns! She hated to think she was betraying him even in her thoughts. It was because of this that she rose as hastily from her bed as she had flung herself across it and began preparing haphazardly for dinner. She had been so sure, after Slade, that she would never care for anyone again, yet Matt, with his warm companionship and gentle, undemanding kisses, had shown her that nothing was impossible. He had revived her faith in mankind, as well as herself, and eventually she had decided she was over Slade and agreed to marry him. Matt could give her a happy life and security. His income would never be in the same bracket as Slade's, with his companies spread all over the world and new ones springing up like mushrooms. But she didn't want diamonds and furs and the life-style that went with them any more. She wanted a settled home and a man willing to make the same commitment as herself to have one. She had changed, and if Slade was back and they did happen to meet she hoped he would realise it.

A quick bath refreshed her and because it was late she wasted no time over the rest of her toilet. After pulling on a short, silky dress, she hurriedly brushed and combed her hair and didn't bother with make-up. Her skin was so pure and creamy she didn't really need any, but sometimes she wished nature hadn't been quite so generous regarding her colouring. Dark red hair was fairly ordinary, but hers seemed to gleam with silken lights, while her eyes, instead of being just an ordinary blue, were more of an intensely vivid violet. Slade had been fascinated by them; he used to say they changed colour according to the mood she was in.

Swiftly Lee's dark winged brows drew together and her delicate little nostrils distended slightly above a full, soft mouth as she rebuked herself impatiently for continuing to think of him. Firmly she directed her thoughts towards her mother. Her mother had always said Lee looked like her with a bit of her French father thrown in. Lee had only been five when her father had been killed, and though she could vaguely remember talking to him, she had no recollection whatsoever as to what he had looked like. Neither could she recall what they had talked about, but she had always held it as proof of how close they had been that she was able to speak good French, while her mother had never mastered the language with anything like the same degree of fluency. Her mother had always poured scorn on her husband's relations and refused to let Lee have anything to do with them, but that hadn't stopped Lee from being curious about them. That was why, after she had fled from Slade in Paris, instead of returning to London she had gone south, intending to seek them out. Unfortunately her plans had come to nothing. En route for the Dordogne, she had met with an accident and when she had come round in a convent hospital, minus her memory, the nuns had mistaken her for one of their own countrywomen because of her fluent French. It hadn't been until she recovered her memory, several months later, that they had discovered the truth and allowed her to come home.

A door banging in the distance made Lee suddenly aware of the devious path her thoughts had taken. She was glad to be brought back to reality, for she had had no intention of going over that period of her life again. Swiftly she left her room to join the others in the lounge, despairing that the sight of a man who merely reminded her of Slade could disturb her so much as to bring back the past, which was surely better forgotten!

She found her three friends idly watching television.

'Matt's late,' Julia greeted her, while Nigel, noticing the slight strain in her eyes, asked quietly if he could get her a sherry.

Guiltily, Lee realised she had forgotten about Matt. 'He must have got held up,' she frowned, after thanking Nigel gratefully.

Just then the phone rang. 'Shall I get it?' offered Sandra, jumping to her feet.

'No, it must be Matt,' Lee replied quickly. 'I may as well go myself.'

Sandra didn't sit down again but left the lounge with her. 'If it is Matt,' she said, 'tell him his favourite dinner will be ruined if he leaves it much longer.'

Lee smiled at her sympathetically as she picked up the telephone in the hall. 'River Bend,' she said crisply.

It was Matt, and when she enquired anxiously what was keeping him, he answered ruefully, 'I'm sorry, darling, I'm afraid I can't make it this evening. You won't have heard, but my cousin Slade's back and he wants to see me.'

Shock raced through Lee like a thousand stampeding horses. It was a terrible blow that her former fears had not been unfounded. She wanted to scream in defiance against a remorseless fate, yet she knew she couldn't do a thing. That Matt claimed a closer relationship with Slade than actually existed, told her he was as impressed as most people by him. It wasn't, of course, something she hadn't been aware of. A faint anger stirred through the shock blanketing her brain, but she was relieved when Matt related her lengthening silence to disappointment.

'I really am sorry, dear,' he repeated hastily, 'but it's not something I feel I should pass up. Slade's put a lot of work my way and I don't think we can afford to offend him.'

'But, Matt,' she protested tautly, 'surely if you explained that you had a date with your fiancée? Does he,' she swallowed hard, 'know about us?'

Matt laughed. 'Slade's always had a funny way of knowing everything that's going on. I'd be willing to bet he knows about us. If he doesn't I'm certainly going to tell him.'

'You don't have to, do you?'

'I feel I should,' Matt replied slowly, obviously wondering why she sounded distraught. 'He's family, after all.'

Lee brushed back a curl from a brow surprisingly damp with perspiration. 'Not that close, surely!'

Matt hesitated, clearly turning things over in his legal mind. 'You used to be friendly with him once, didn't you? Didn't you go to London with his mother or something . . .?'

'Yes,' she broke in quickly, hoping to divert him, 'a long time ago.'

Matt didn't seem to notice the hoarseness of her voice. 'Then you must realise he's not a man who would give me a second chance. He could have enough lined up to give us an excellent start in life, and if I refuse to see him, this evening, he might not want to see me again.'

Lee's heart sank as she tensely considered Matt's warning. There would be no second chance for her, she knew that, if Slade learned that she was engaged to his cousin. If he still harboured thoughts of revenge, he wouldn't hesitate to destroy her engagement with all the ruthlessness he was capable of. 'Do we need his— patronage that much?' she whispered.

'Darling,' Matt sighed, forever patient, 'if I hadn't had so much to do for my family, you know I'd have been in a different position.'

'I understand, Matt,' she soothed automatically. Matt's parents had suffered a long period of ill-health. There had been private operations to pay for, and, on top of this, his mother had got badly in debt. Matt helped them, as that was the way he was made, but it had done nothing for his bank balance.

'Will you call later?' she asked, not able to decide whether she wanted him to or not. He would naturally be full of Slade—how he looked, what he was doing, what he'd said, and she couldn't be sure she was ready for that yet.

Matt settled her fears, giving temporary if not permanent relief. 'It might be foolish to say yes and then not turn up.'

'I'll see you tomorrow, then,' she said quickly.

'You can count on it,' he assured her lovingly.

'Matt can't make it,' was all the explanation she gave as she followed her friends into the kitchen for dinner. They usually ate in the kitchen as it was huge and contained a large table and saved heating the dining-room.

'Business or personal?' asked Julia dryly, having her own opinion of Matt's family problems, which weren't exactly a well-kept secret.

Surprisingly it was Sandra who sprang to his defence. 'Is it his fault that his parents expect too much of him? It's not really their fault either,' she rushed on. 'His father takes a lot of looking after and his mother gets tired out and does foolish things. All she needs is a firm hand.'

Seeing how Sandra was almost glaring at Lee, even if Lee wasn't conscious of it, Julia intervened hastily, 'You can't expect Lee to risk alienating her future mother-in-law.'

'I'm not suggesting she goes as far as that!' Sandra retorted hotly. 'Half Mrs Leland's troubles are simply a cry for help, and she's a nice woman, one couldn't be hard on her.'

Lee, her thoughts certainly not with the Lelands, whatever their troubles, heard the argument passing to and fro over her head without being aware of its exact content. After the meal, when Julia stunned them all, including Nigel, by agreeing to go out with him, she retreated to her room and tried to catch up on a little writing.

At ten, still facing a blank page, she gave up, yet she couldn't think of going to bed, the house seemed to be suffocating her. Quickly changing into a pair of jeans, she ran downstairs to find Sandra.

'I'm going out on my bike for an hour,' she told the other girl, who had returned to the TV in the lounge. Impulsively she asked, as Sandra looked lonely, 'Why don't you come? We could find a Coke somewhere.'

'No, thank you,' Sandra refused primly, as if she had never enjoyed riding pillion. 'Anyway,' she added more graciously, 'someone ought to stay here just in case Matt does turn up and he's hungry.'

Lee agreed, 'Yes, perhaps,' knowing she couldn't sound much like a newly engaged girl missing her fiancé. She did love Matt—she did, she assured herself fiercely, leaving Sandra to go outside. If Slade's unexpected return had numbed her normal feelings, it wasn't to say that they weren't there any more. Once she was used to the idea of his being back, she would soon readjust. Besides, he might not stay long.

Summer was slipping slowly into autumn, giving warm, lazy days but hazy nights. This evening fog lay like a shroud along the river bank, making the night appear darker than it actually was. Ignoring her car, Lee wheeled her Honda from the garage again. Sometimes, when something inside her seemed to be crying out for release, a burst of speed helped. No other way seemed to work.

She was about to close the garage doors behind her when a sudden noise made her start. Straining her eyes, she managed to make out a small, thin figure. 'Oh, Trigg!' she exclaimed sharply. 'What on earth are you doing here?'

It was Trigg Mansfield, a neighbour's child. The dismay in Lee's voice was caused by the fact that he was only eight years old and asthmatic and his home was three miles away.

As she stared at him incredulously, Trigg advanced unrepentantly from his hiding place. 'I just wanted to take a look at your bike,' he grinned disarmingly. 'Mum and Dad are out, so they won't miss me.'

'Oh, Trigg!' Lee wasn't sure whom she felt the more exasperated with, him or his parents. The Mansfields usually just went as far as the nearest pub or hotel for a drink, but she couldn't believe it was wise to leave a rather frail, eight-year-old boy in the house after dark by himself. Especially one as ready to take advantage of such a situation as Trigg!

'You really ought to go home, love,' she told him helplessly.

'I'd get there much quicker if you took me,' he replied craftily, and looking into his eager little face Lee hadn't the heart to let him see she saw through his very obvious machinations.

It was caution that made her hesitate. 'Shouldn't I try and discover if your parents are home first? If I gave them a ring they could come and fetch you.'

His face crumpled with disappointment. 'Oh, Lee, no! They won't be there anyway,' he added dully.

She gave in. After all, he was taking her mind off other things, so maybe she owed him something. And he didn't have much of a life. His mother was highly strung and his father too easy-going. Neither provided the kind of stable relationship that Trigg was in need of at the moment.

'I should use the car,' she frowned.

'I don't like cars,' he said stubbornly, looking so yearningly at her bike that Lee's heart ached for him.

'Come on, then,' she sighed, hoping she wouldn't live to regret it. He let her fix her spare helmet over his thick fair curls. It fitted well, which should ensure his safety, and he had ridden with her before.

'That's it, trooper,' she smiled, making a final adjustment to the strap. 'Mind you, I'm just going carefully—no speeding.'

She would have been speeding if she had been on her own, but with Trigg sitting behind her she didn't even think about it. She was going very carefully indeed when, unfortunately, the bulb in her front light failed, which plunged her into darkness and made it impossible for the car sweeping around the corner to see her. The bright beam of powerful headlights caught her full in the face, blinding her, sending her skidding on to the grass verge. Even so, they might have been all right if

she hadn't hit an open gutter. The impact spelled
immediate disaster as it made the bike practically stand
on end as it came to a sudden stop. Mercifully, Trigg
merely slid fairly gently off the back, but Lee landed in
the ditch with the bike on top of her.

Struggling from under it, she was more concerned for
Trigg than herself and paid scant attention to the car
that had screeched to a halt a few yards away. She
didn't even bother to glance at the driver, who had
slammed from his vehicle in a storm of rage and
impatience.

'Of all the brainless things to do!' he snapped. 'You
could have been killed!'

Lee's whole body stiffened as she bent over a dazed
Trigg. She would have known that voice anywhere!
Fearing she was going to faint, she wrenched off her
helmet, hoping Slade wouldn't recognise her. She felt a
return of the shock she had experienced that afternoon,
but the volume of it was far greater. Perhaps the near-
collision she had had would account for some of it, but
she was sure she had been no more than slightly shaken
until Slade appeared. A terrible sickness rose in her
throat and she trembled violently. Matt had confirmed
that Slade was back, but nothing had prepared her for
the trauma of meeting him again. Hugging Trigg to her,
she didn't know whether she was comforting him or
using him as a shield.

She was grateful for the darkness. Once Slade would
have known her anywhere, but it had been over five
years. She tried to control the heavy beat of her heart so
she could speak. 'My lights failed,' she managed
hoarsely. 'It wasn't my fault.'

There was an abrupt silence. She heard him draw a
sharp breath. His eyes glinted as she lifted her head, she
could feel them boring into her.

'My God, it's you!' he exclaimed thickly.

Lee felt too shattered to reply immediately. His face
was shadowed, she could just make him out, but if she

had had any doubts about his identity they disappeared when he reached swiftly down to draw Trigg and her to their feet.

'You don't think I tried to stop you on purpose?' she gasped angrily, as incredibly familiar sensations began flooding through her.

'I shouldn't think so,' he replied more smoothly. 'Anyway, we can discuss that later. It's more important, right now, to make sure that neither of you is injured.'

'It's not your fault that we aren't!' she muttered fiercely. 'You were driving too fast.'

'I told you to leave it, Lee,' he said harshly. 'Let's take a look at your young friend.'

'I'm all right, sir,' Trigg assured him stolidly, suddenly finding his voice. 'I just got a little bump.'

Not taking his word for it, Slade ran his hands lightly over him. 'You seem all right, but you must have got a fright, all the same. How old are you?'

'Eight.'

Slade straightened, his eyes on Lee again. 'You don't change, do you? You're still irresponsible and you still have that infernal machine.'

'It passes its M.O.T.'

'And you still ride as recklessly,' he continued as if she had never spoken. 'I thought you would have grown up by now!'

Grown up! Lee shuddered. He had a nerve! Hadn't he seen to it personally that she had grown up five years ago? 'I don't have time to stand here enjoying your insults,' she retorted tightly. 'I have to get Trigg home before his parents discover he's missing.'

'Enough!' snapped Slade, as if he had heard all he wanted to hear. To Trigg he said, 'You can count yourself lucky, this time, but don't let me catch you on Lee's motorbike again. Now I'll take you home, wherever that might be.'

'The Willows,' Trigg muttered, beginning to cry.

Lee put a protective arm round him, but Slade

bundled them both straight into his car. He took no
notice of either Lee's anger or the boy's tears, and Lee's
anger increased at his high-handed behaviour. He might
accuse her of not changing, but surely he hadn't
changed himself! He still believed only what it suited
him to believe. He was arrogant and overbearing, bent
on having his own way. She stared at his dark profile,
the set of his wide shoulders, and kept on trying to
convince herself that she hated him.

He asked for brief directions and she gave them to him,
then rubbed the back of her hand wearily over her brow.

'How are you feeling?' The words seemed torn out of
him and she saw his mouth tighten.

'Fine,' she muttered, not quite truthfully. 'I don't
know why you bother to ask.'

Slade Western didn't either. He didn't like the way
she affected him after over five years of pretending
rigorously she didn't exist. She had cut through the
careful control he had built up with one glance from
those fabulous blue eyes. If anything she was more
beautiful than he remembered. When she had looked at
him, even after all this time, he had been stunned by his
own powerful reaction. And she'd had the nerve to
forget him and get involved with Matt! It was for
Matt's sake that he had hurried home immediately he
had heard of the engagement.

'It's a question I might put to anyone who's had a
recent scrape with death,' he retorted curtly.

'You were going too fast!' she parroted, as the car
seemed to hurtle forward. 'You're doing it again!'

'I'm in complete control. If I had been going too
fast,' he pointed out with maddening logic, 'how could I
have stopped so quickly?'

Defeated, Lee lapsed into silence. Trigg huddled
against her, his thin body curiously pathetic, his need of
reassurance clearly as great as her own.

'I hope they won't be back,' he whimpered. 'I'm
scared they might be mad at me.'

She knew he was referring to his parents. 'I'll explain everything,' she whispered soothingly, 'Don't worry.'

He gulped but tried to smile as Slade drew up by a small house just off the road. Lee saw the door burst open almost before the car had stopped and wished Trigg hadn't suddenly chosen that moment to burst into tears again. It was just reaction, but she knew Dulcie Mansfield would put a far worse construction on it.

'Trigg!' the distraught mother cried, almost snatching him from Lee's arms as she helped him from the car. 'Oh, darling,' she wailed, 'wherever have you been? I've been worried out of my mind!'

It seemed unlikely that Dulcie had been home many minutes herself, because she was still clutching her handbag. George, her husband, hurried after her, but he wasn't in nearly such a state.

He displayed more irritation than anxiety as he spoke to his son. 'You left your bedroom door open, or I should never have known you weren't there.'

'I'm sorry,' Lee started to explain, 'I'm afraid we had a slight accident.'

'Accident!' shrieked Dulcie, her voice rising wildly, eyes wide. 'How . . .? Where?'

'I—well . . .' stammered Lee, not in the best condition to cope with Dulcie's hysterics. 'I was bringing him home on my bike and we—er—met Mr Western on a bend . . .'

Slade had left the car but had made no attempt to come to Lee's assistance. Neither did he make any effort to either deny or admit his part in the affair. He just stood there, looking so dark and striking that Dulcie's eyes continued to widen like saucers as she caught sight of him.

'You mean—you crashed into—him?' She did a pretty little swoon, conveniently into her husband's arms, apparently quite overcome.

Lee watched in mute fascination. Dulcie had once

been an aspiring actress, but after six months at a
London drama school had decided that marriage
wouldn't be nearly such hard work as acting. Marriage
didn't, however, stop her from practising at home the
career she still hankered after but which her fundamental laziness had disallowed her from taking up. At
parties she managed to faint quite regularly and
frequently caused sensational little fiascos in shops and
other public places. Slade would know nothing of this,
of course. To him, Dulcie must seem merely a
distressed, badly done by mother.

'We didn't crash into him,' Lee said quickly as Dulcie
opened her eyes. 'I ran on to the grass verge.'

'Oh, my God!' Dulcie moaned. 'My son, my only
child, might have been killed!'

'I wasn't,' said Trigg, very earnestly.

'Dulcie!' George frowned. 'Trigg looks all right to
me. I'm sure Lee didn't mean anything to happen.'

'You would stick up for her!' Dulcie spat. 'You'd let
her get away with murder, just because you think she's
the most beautiful thing on two legs!'

'Dulcie!' George appealed again, his colour deepening
even in the poor light. 'That has nothing to do with it.
Now shut up, there's a good girl, and just let's get Trigg
inside.'

'He'll still have to see a doctor,' Dulcie cried.

'I don't need to, Mum, really!' protested Trigg. 'I just
fell off gently.'

'Oh, no!' Dulcie went on moaning weakly. 'How can
you be sure?'

'I think a warm drink should be enough,' said Lee,
with the intention of coming to Trigg's rescue.

'You would, wouldn't you!' Dulcie retorted bitterly.
'You wouldn't want the publicity . . .'

George, moving decisively for once, took a firm hold
of his wife and son. 'If Trigg is any the worse, it won't
help him standing here.'

As he hustled them inside, Lee saw Dulcie's eyes

gravitate in Slade's direction. 'I can't thank you enough for bringing Trigg home, Mr Western.'

'My pleasure,' Slade returned gravely.

Lee called after them, 'I'll ring in the morning.'

'Nice people,' Slade mused as they got back in the car. 'New neighbours?'

'They've been here three years,' she replied shortly.

He draped a seat belt around her and she wondered why she was letting him. At the touch of his hands she shivered. 'I can manage,' she exclaimed, jerking from him, wishing she didn't suspect he was enjoying himself.

He took little notice of her protests. To her dismay, as she finished fastening her seat-belt, he reached for her, sliding his hands up her arms to cup her face.

'Still angry with me?'

Lee didn't think he was referring to the events of the past hour, and something seemed to explode in her brain. 'You haven't been back five minutes,' she snapped, 'and all I've heard is you're still this, that and the other! You condemn me out of hand like you always did. You ask questions and still supply your own answers. Well, I might never have been an angel, but you were certainly never a saint! And do you realise,' she rushed on, barely pausing for breath, 'that the Mansfield's outside light is on, and if they cared to look out, I'd rather not dwell on what they might think.'

'You aren't in my arms—not yet anyway.' Mockingly he traced the full outline of her indignant lips with sensuous fingers.

'Nor likely to be,' she retorted, trying to find strength to finally push him away. She knew what he meant, but she didn't mean to respond. If he was here for a few weeks and looking for someone to amuse himself with, then he'd better look elsewhere!

He gazed at her for a long moment while powerful emotions raged through her. She felt torn in a thousand different directions. Could she hope that this man would leave her in peace to enjoy her new-found, fragile happiness?

As if he had read her thoughts, Slade released her, but caught the hand her engagement ring was on. His silky voice warned her of what was coming almost before he spoke. 'This was a mistake, you know. Getting engaged to Matt wasn't a very sensible thing to do.'

'He's a nice person,' she grated.

'That's what I'm driving at.' The eyes, so dark a green they might have been black, glinted. 'Too nice for the likes of you.'

She gasped at the insult, her own eyes glittering with some of the same fury that lurked behind his. 'So,' she retaliated recklessly, 'what are you going to do about it?'

She should have remembered how dangerous it was to challenge him. He smiled, but she sensed the steel under the indestructible charm. 'You and I have to talk.'

Her throat felt hot because she knew he was about to trap her into making a promise to see him again. Whatever happened, she mustn't have anything more to do with him. He was soft-pedalling until he thought he had her exactly where he wanted her. And that might only be the beginning!

# CHAPTER TWO

SUDDENLY realising she was staring at him apprehensively, Lee swiftly pulled her hand from his and veiled her eyes. Her skin tingled as though it had been burned, but she resisted the impulse to clench her scorched fingers.

'I don't think we have anything to talk about,' she replied coldly. 'I'd be grateful if you'd just drop me off beside my bike and leave me. There can't be much point in seeing each other again.'

'I shouldn't have suggested it if I hadn't been sure it was absolutely necessary,' he retorted suavely. 'But I can see you're too shaken to be reasonable tonight.' Slipping the car in gear, he turned back on to the road. 'I'll take you home, but that monstrosity you persist in riding can stay where it is. You must have enough bruises without adding to them unnecessarily.'

Lee opened her mouth to argue, then closed it again. Anything to get away from him! Alone with him, she didn't feel safe, and the past few hours had been altogether too much. She didn't have to pretend to feel ill. A dreadful nausea was rising in her throat and the shaken feeling inside her was making her increasingly aware that she wasn't as immune to the man by her side as she had imagined herself to be. He could still make her pulses race alarmingly.

He drove past the spot where her bike lay in the ditch without sparing it even a brief glance. Lee wasn't overconcerned, she could collect it in the morning. The frame was probably twisted, she was sure no one was going to run away with it and she was reluctant to accept any more assistance from Slade. The sooner they parted company the better she would like it.

Outside River Bend his tyres scraped on the gravel as
he drew up. 'Thank you,' she said huskily, jumping out
and running towards the house.

Leaping from the car after her, he caught her arm,
halting her swift flight. 'Not so fast!' he said ruthlessly.

Lee stiffened, wishing he wasn't so tall that he seemed
to tower over her. He was six foot two and powerfully
built; his leanness was deceptive. He packed a lot of
muscle. As he tightened his hold she stood beside him
submissively, knowing from past experience that to
attempt to fight him physically was well-nigh impossible.

'I'm tired, Slade,' she kept her eyes focussed on a
point just below his shoulder. 'And a bit sore. I'm only
beginning to realise.'

His eyes blazed in the darkness. 'You were under that
bike, you little fool. I have no wish to repeat myself, but
you're still as reckless and irresponsible as you used to
be. You could have killed both yourself and that boy.
Why do you do it, Lee?'

'I'm not irresponsible!' she cried, feeling forced to
spring to her own defence. 'Trigg was hiding in the
garage when I went for my bike. He begged me to take
him home . . .'

'Haven't you a car?'

'Yes.'

'Then why didn't you use it?' He shook her slightly,
as if he couldn't help himself. 'You're still . . .'

Lee broke in angrily, trying to ignore a sense of guilt,
'I wish you'd remove that word from your vocabulary.
I'm tired of hearing it!'

Looking preoccupied, he took no notice of what she
was saying. 'Why were you going out on your own at
that time of night? Matt wasn't available. Had you
arranged to meet someone else?'

'How dare you!' she spluttered, longing to smack the
contemptuous mockery from his face. 'I never had your
insatiable appetite!'

'God,' he breathed, 'time can't have distorted your memory as much as all that!'

She flushed, a painful red. 'You exaggerate with your horrible insinuations. Anyway, why drag things up?'

His eyes went as hard as the chiselled bones of his face. 'It's only for the sake of others that I'm dragging things up, as you put it. Matt could never match you.'

Oh, she fumed inwardly, why was he doing this to her? Saying such things! Couldn't he leave her alone? 'You're trying to make out I was as bad as you were!'

He stared at her, his hard mouth suddenly amused. 'Think about it when you get to bed.'

'I'm going there,' she retorted furiously, 'as soon as you let me, but certainly not to think about you!'

The lazy amusement went out of his face and he looked at her with savage anger, his eyes biting. 'I put my brand on you and never gave you permission to remove it. I'll be calling to see you very soon. You'd better be in and prepared to listen.'

'What were you doing here today?' she asked, her mind spinning.

Between his teeth he muttered, 'You saw me?'

'I thought I did, this afternoon.'

'You could have been right,' he replied shortly. 'I was in the vicinity. This evening I was on my way to see you.'

Lee said bitterly, 'I had a date with Matt this evening, but he rang and told me he couldn't make it. He said you wanted to see him to discuss business. Did you also take the opportunity to tell him about us?'

'No,' Slade looked at her levelly with a cold smile. 'I assumed you might have told him yourself, when he asked you to marry him. Anyway,' he shrugged, 'why should I risk alienating myself from Matt when there are other ways of achieving what I came for?'

'Well,' she said carefully, staring at him suspiciously, 'if you didn't mention anything to Matt, how is it he didn't come straight to River Bend after your meeting was over?'

'There are one or two things I want from him, first thing in the morning.' He ran a bland finger down her smooth cheek. 'I was sure you would understand.'

The man was a monster! Lee knew another urge to strike him. He had deliberately prevented Matt from coming to see her. Looking into his face, she was sure that was true. He was impervious to all but his own desires, his face a mask of steely authority. The dark eyes held menace and unmistakable, unyielding will-power. But she wasn't beaten yet! Belligerently she ignored the shivery sensation creeping over the hot skin he so mockingly caressed. Jerking her head back, she said tersely. 'Listen, Slade! You can no longer interfere in my life, and I'll thank you to keep out of it.'

He smiled, and her heart was suddenly racing as his mouth swooped to crush down relentlessly on her parted lips. For a moment, before she wrenched away from him, Lee, terrifyingly, lost all sense of what she was doing. The thick, warm darkness into which she fell was like going back in time and place. Something spiralled crazily inside her. She heard the intake of his breath as his arms jerked her to him and their bodies met in searing impact an instant before she forced herself from him.

Slade's dark eyes had a glitter in them and though he made no attempt to stop her this time when she fled, the voice that followed her held more than a hint of triumph. 'You ask the impossible, Lee, and if you don't know it you soon will.'

Lee almost beat her pillow to pulp that night before she got to sleep, and no sooner did she seem to close her eyes than Julia was there, waking her up.

'You've overslept,' she said with a concerned frown. 'It's so unlike you that I felt I had to come and see if anything was wrong before I went to work.'

'Oh!' Lee moaned as the events of the previous

evening returned to overwhelm her. She stared at Julia blindly.

'Something is wrong!' Julia exclaimed sharply.

Swiftly Lee pulled herself together and somehow, after explaining briefly about the accident, managed to convince Julia that she was none the worse. 'I wasn't going fast, neither was the car, and the ditch was well padded with grass,' she ended with a wry grimace.

Julia looked faintly intrigued. 'Who was this man who rescued you? Was he nice?' she asked.

Lee, having inadvertently implied that Slade was a stranger, impulsively decided not to correct the impression. 'Not so you'd notice,' she replied shortly. 'He certainly wasn't sympathetic.'

Julia guessed shrewdly. 'He blamed you?'

'Naturally,' Lee returned tightly.

'Some men can't bear to think they're at fault when a woman is involved,' observed Julia dryly. 'If no one was actually hurt, I shouldn't dwell on it too much.'

Lee threw back the sheets. 'I suppose I'd better get up and go and rescue my poor old bike before someone reports it to the police.' She didn't want to talk about Slade any more than was necessary.

Julia's glance went over her anxiously. 'Are you sure you're really fit enough? It can't have been much fun having a motor-bike landing on top of you, even one as light as yours.'

'I do have a few bruises,' admitted Lee with a shrug, 'but that's all.'

A car tooted in the drive below, interrupting their conversation. 'Nigel's getting impatient,' Julia's cheeks were suddenly slightly pink. 'My car isn't going too well, so he offered to run me to work.'

'Ah!' grinned Lee.

Julia retreated hastily from her teasing smile. 'See you later. Mind you . . .' she turned in the doorway, 'if you don't feel so good, after you're up, I should go back to bed, if I were you, and call your doctor.'

Lee had no intention of following Julia's advice, but she was surprised to find how stiff she was. The parts of her that were bruised were sore too. Slade must have been right when he said she'd been lucky. She realised this, of course, and she might not have argued with him if he had been a little kinder. Her eyes filled with anger as she remembered he had given her many things in the past, but seldom kindness. He had been generous, but never with his affections. Passion was the only emotion she had ever aroused in him, that and possessiveness. He was a selfish swine. He had never pretended to care two hoots for her, yet he had been capable of becoming almost violent if she had so much as looked at another man.

Aware that she was trembling and that her reflection showed her pale and heavy-eyed, Lee resolutely thrust all thoughts of Slade from her mind. For years she had managed not to think of him. It shouldn't be too difficult to forget him, this morning, even though he was back.

Slipping on an old woollen dressing-gown, she went downstairs to make some tea. She loved having guests, but she also liked those hours of the day when she had the house to herself. The large old rooms were quiet, soothing to her pounding head, and she glanced through open doorways appreciatively as she made her way to the kitchen. Her grandfather had only had the house to leave her, but she would rather have had the house than anything else. She could have used some money to refurbish it, though. It grieved her that it was growing shabby through lack of funds.

She had just switched the kettle on when Matt called. The front door wasn't locked and he walked straight in. Hearing him behind her, Lee turned with a start. 'You're early!' she exclaimed.

He kissed her gently, noting the surprise in her eyes. 'I didn't knock,' he explained. 'I thought you might be in bed.'

'In bed?' she echoed, clearly puzzled.

His glance swept over her anxiously. 'Slade rang, first thing. He told me you'd had an accident.'

'Good heavens,' Lee retorted impatiently, thinking Slade hadn't wasted any time and wondering tensely what he was up to, 'you could hardly call it that!'

'Where's your motor-cycle?' he asked, so offhandedly, she suspected he knew very well where it was!

Her soft mouth tightened. 'In a ditch, about a mile along the road. You must have passed it.'

Matt hesitated and looked hurt as she edged away from the arm he had laid around her shoulders. 'Slade didn't think you'd acted wisely, giving that boy a lift home, and I'm afraid I feel forced to agree with him, Lee.'

'Why?' she asked, her blue eyes stormy. 'Surely it was enough for him that you jumped to do his bidding last night, without criticising your fiancée.'

Reddening uncomfortably, Matt said hastily, 'He only pointed out, Lee, and again I'm inclined to agree with him, that you tend to be a little—er—headstrong.'

Not the words Slade had used, she was sure! 'That sounds like criticism to me!' she retorted shortly, switching off the kettle with a snap as the water boiled and making a pot of tea.

Matt ploughed on earnestly with little of the tact he normally employed in his business. 'He merely meant, if you cause any trouble it could be embarrassing for me.'

Pushing two slices of bread in the toaster, Lee sat down mutinously at the kitchen table. 'How?'

Matt lowered himself opposite carefully, his movements, Lee reflected, disparaging of him for the first time, exactly in keeping with his profession—he never did anything in a hurry. Because she knew that wasn't fair yet felt so mixed up, her hands trembled as she poured tea in their cups.

Noticing, Matt used it to elaborate on what he was trying to explain. 'You see, darling, how the whole thing's affected you, so you can't be surprised that I'm worried about possible repercussions on my practice. The Mansfields are an unpredictable lot, at least she is, and the son isn't strong. If he's the least bit droopy today, she's going to blame you, and she's just the sort to make a drama out of reporting your antics to the media or the police—maybe both.'

'B-but she couldn't!' Lee stammered hollowly, her anger changing to dismay as she stared at him. 'Could she?'

'That remains to be seen,' Matt muttered gloomily. 'Even if she doesn't there'll be rumours, which might not do my practice much good.'

'It didn't do me much good either,' she retorted bitterly, thinking she'd just about had enough of self-centred men. Slade, when he had forced her to live with him, had always refused to consider her side of their relationship, while Matt, for all he had learned she had had an accident, had yet to ask if she had been hurt or was recovered. He was more worried over any damage she might have done to his reputation!

His manner changed, though, almost as soon as she spoke. 'Oh, sweetheart!' he groaned, reaching over the table to squeeze her hand contritely. 'You can't believe that I came here this morning only concerned for myself. When Slade rang and told me what had happened I got a terrible shock.'

Lee felt like retorting that it wasn't very evident, but instead she attacked Slade. 'Slade Western has no business interfering in our affairs!'

'He's just trying to be helpful, dear,' Matt protested, frowning on her hot face. 'He seems to imagine that a solicitor's wife should be beyond reproach. Of course that might just have to do with his being my cousin. He's always had a kind of chip on his shoulder regarding family respectability.'

She didn't ask why, for once she had asked Slade himself and got no answer. 'Has it ever occurred to you, Matt, that Slade might not like me?' she asked.

Letting go of her hand, Matt returned to his toast, munching worriedly. 'I'm sure he likes you. How could he not?' he added, with an astonishing lack of logic, 'when you're so beautiful.'

'He might not consider that any recommendation!' she said tartly.

Matt studied her, to her amazement as if he was actually considering this. 'You're very flamboyant,' he eventually muttered awkwardly, just when Lee was beginning to wonder what was coming. 'Even in that old robe you'd stand out in a crowd. Perhaps, while Slade is here, it might help if you could manage to look more—er—like—well, Sandra. Tone down a bit, you know?'

Sandra always looked cool and remote, very dignified. Lee knew what Matt meant, but that didn't stop her from feeling furious. 'Slade's not been here five minutes, Matt, and already he's coming between us! And,' she added somewhat illogically, 'I don't see how he can criticise you when his own reputation can't be spotless.'

Matt stirred uncomfortably. 'Well, he does have affairs—after all, he's thirty-six and unmarried, but they're always conducted discreetly . . .'

Did Matt think he was telling her something she didn't already know? Angrily Lee glared at him, then calmed down. He admired Slade, and who was she to disillusion him? Slade's life was a human record of brilliant achievement. If there were any skeletons in his cupboards they firmly remained there; he guarded both his business and personal reputation almost fanatically.

She sighed, realising suddenly that Matt and she were nearly quarrelling and she might be playing right into Slade's hands. 'I'll give Dulcie Mansfield a ring this morning,' she promised, changing the subject abruptly, 'and see how things are. If she threatens to make a fuss, I could point out that leaving an eight-year-old in the house on his own, night after night, isn't likely to be approved of by the authorities.'

Matt's relieved expression was marred by a frown. 'You'd have to do it tactfully. I know you're fond of the boy, but Dulcie's his mother.'

'You don't have to remind me,' Lee said wryly.

Glancing at his watch reluctantly, Matt stood up. 'I have an appointment in half an hour—I must dash.'

Lee watched him silently as he adjusted his jacket and ran a quick hand over his hair. In his own way he was as impressive as Slade, though not so tall or well built. He was older than Slade and their characters were completely different. Usually Matt was quiet and rarely made a move before he had thought it over, whereas Slade made decisions with a snap of his fingers and it was doubtful if he had ever worried over anything in his life. It was important, she thought desperately, that he shouldn't be allowed to hurt or damage in any way the harmonious relationship which Matt and she had so painstakingly built up.

'Will I see you this evening?' she smiled, after Matt had asked a few searching if belated questions regarding her health.

He nodded as he bent to kiss her briefly. 'Slade said you should rest, but I'll probably look in, in any case, just to make sure you are.'

He did return that evening, though he was late and it had nothing to do with Slade this time. Not directly, anyway, he assured her. Slade had given him a lot to do, but once he managed to fit this in with the work he already had on hand, everything should be a lot easier.

Matt looked so tired that Lee hadn't the heart to wonder aloud why Slade should suddenly discover he was apparently essential for the continued smooth running of his business. Slade had legal advisers all over the place, from what she could remember. As she had done earlier, she suppressed a mounting urgency to ask Matt if he knew how long Slade would be staying. It wasn't the question she was frightened of, it was the answer. She had no desire to hear that he might be here for a longer time than she might consider endurable.

Having had a rather unsettling day herself, she was content to leave Sandra to fuss over Matt, serving his dinner, which they had kept hot, then coffee in the lounge. She wasn't even consciously aware of how Sandra continued fluttering tenderly around him, her eyes only leaving him occasionally to rest disapprovingly on Lee, who she had clearly decided was lacking in sympathy for her fiancé.

After rescuing her bike which, contrary to her expectations, was little the worse, Lee had got out her car and paid the Mansfields a visit. She had wanted to see that Trigg was all right and felt she couldn't rely on what Dulcie might tell her over the phone.

Dulcie, surprisingly, after her ill-concealed antagonism of the night before, had no complaints. Lee had expected her to be full of them. Trigg had gone off to school as usual, she said, while she and George had almost recovered from the shock they had received. George had made Trigg promise he would never go out by himself again after dark. It wasn't until Dulcie offered her a sherry and began plying her with questions about Slade that Lee understood why she was being so pleasant. Somehow she had managed to cope brilliantly with Dulcie's curiosity, leaving her satisfied without giving much away.

Returning home, she had been too nervous over Slade's threatened visit to settle down to work. Knowing her publisher was waiting for her next book hadn't helped to make her mind less blank. Eventually she had given up trying to write, and, ignoring her aching body, started to clean the house. Yet, though physical exertion brought a certain relief, the threat of a knock on the door had always been with her. Only now, with Matt and her friends all about her, did she feel comparatively safe.

She was even beginning to relax when Nigel arrived home at ten. He had rung earlier and said he didn't know what time he would be in.

'Sorry I'm late, folks,' he grimaced wearily, 'but maybe I'm lucky to be here at all. The big boss is back and it's been twelve hours of non-stop consultations. You'd hardly recognise the place—there's quite a different atmosphere.'

You can say that again! Lee thought hollowly as he almost echoed her own words to Matt. She felt even more shattered as Nigel, enjoying the attention he was getting, continued, 'He intends staying until the new project we're developing gets under way, instead of keeping an eye on its progress as he usually does from abroad.'

Lee, feeling herself growing cold all over, heard Julia ask curiously, 'Will he commute from London?'

'I don't think so.' Nigel collapsed in a chair, accepting a cup of coffee from her with a grateful smile as he replied. 'I believe his mother's with him and they're re-opening the old family house on the river. Rumour has it that there's going to be a grand ball or barbecue or something, and we're all invited.'

'How exciting!' exclaimed Sandra.

'It is, all round,' he grinned enthusiastically, then sighed. 'It makes me wish I'd taken my holiday a week earlier instead of this weekend. Although,' he hastened, glancing happily at Julia, 'if I had taken it then, maybe you wouldn't have agreed to come with me.'

If Julia's face had been pink that morning in Lee's room, it was red now. 'I was going to tell you,' she said defensively, glancing around the ring of surprised faces. 'I only decided a few hours ago.'

'When I rang at six,' Nigel put in triumphantly, gazing at Julia, not concealing the fact that he adored her.

Sandra and Matt began teasing them unmercifully, but Lee restrained herself to an interested smile. She was happy for Nigel, but if Julia's feelings for him were still fragile, she didn't want to put any strain on them and risk spoiling anything.

She felt her attitude might be right when after a minute Julia said to Sandra rather sharply, 'We're going on holiday, not a honeymoon. We both have two weeks to take and we fancied the same place, so it seemed silly not to go together.'

'Where are you going?' Sandra asked quickly, sensitive enough to realise she might have been a bit tactless.

'Venice!' breathed Julia, her sweet face composed again. 'You've never wanted to go there, but I always have, and it's not a place I should enjoy on my own. I mean,' she smiled at Lee, 'imagine visiting the Doges' Palace or seeing all the palaces lining the Grand Canal and having no one to marvel with. It might just about kill me!'

Matt glanced lazily at Lee, putting out a hand to touch her auburn hair as she sat beside him. 'You haven't had a holiday this year, Lee.'

Apprehensive that he was about to suggest they should go off together, as well, without wondering why she had no wish to holiday with him, she said quickly, 'I shan't bother this year—maybe next.'

'That will be your honeymoon, surely?' grinned Nigel, despite Julia's discouraging frown.

'It will be.' Lee laid a quick hand on Matt's arm, immediately thinking of Slade. Whatever happened he wasn't going to interfere with her plans! She loved Matt, and if Slade didn't consider she was good enough for him, surely that was for Matt to decide?

Sleep didn't come to Lee any easier that night than it had done the night before. She was tired, but it was her mind, not her body that wouldn't let her rest. It was full of thoughts of Slade which she couldn't get rid of. Even when Matt had kissed her goodnight, she had felt his presence, as if he had actually been there, standing beside them.

This evening, when Slade hadn't turned up and she had begun to believe his threats had been idle ones, she had managed to relax, until Nigel had told them Slade was opening up the house and his mother was with him. Then her tension had returned, worse than ever. Slade never did anything without a purpose. He had new experiments going all over the world; there had to be a specific reason why he should choose to take a special interest in the one at Reading. The old family home might be here, but she couldn't feel convinced that he had developed a sudden nostalgia for it after not bothering with it for years. She had assumed he would be staying at the flat he kept for convenience when he was working late, above the offices at the works. Now to hear that he might be here to stay for several weeks filled her with the kind of dread she had no wish to analyse.

With weary eyes, she lay staring into the darkness, letting a mind that seemed always too eager to dwell on the past have its way at last. Being the only child of a successful Hollywood actress hadn't been easy. Until a few months before her mother died, she had been shuttled back and forth between boarding schools and the equally strict care of a martinet of a housekeeper in Los Angeles. She had been over eighteen before she was allowed to leave school and, even then, her mother had been unhappy about it. She had been frightened of the influence of the film industry on her daughter. 'I don't want you to have anything to do with acting,' she had repeated nearly every day, and threatened to send Lee to live with her grandfather almost as regularly.

Lee had no desire to be a star, but neither had she wanted to leave America to live with her grandfather. After years of having her every movement supervised either by school or her mother's staff, all she could think about was having a little freedom. Reluctantly Liz had given it to her, and Lee had to admit it had gone to her head a little. It had been exciting to discover how

her youth and looks attracted men. For a while she had
enjoyed playing idle if innocent games with them,
enjoying the sense of power which a beautiful face and
body gave her, without in any way committing herself.
Looking back, she often felt surprised that she hadn't
got herself into some kind of trouble. It seemed ironical,
when America was so much bigger than England, and
the dangers, by comparison, so much greater, that
it had been in England where she had finally come to
grief.

It had been several years since she had last seen her
grandfather, but he and Lee's mother had been in no
way estranged. Indeed Ralph Peterson had been proud
of his daughter, it was just that their individual work
had kept them tied to different parts of the world.

Lee wondered now if her mother's death hadn't
affected her grandfather more than she'd thought, but
at just nineteen she had been more interested in her own
reactions to a new environment than her grandfather's
feelings. Once she had stopped grieving for her mother
she soon made friends in the neighbourhood, and the
sort of country-club restaurant which Ralph ran
interested her a lot. While she never had any ambition
to take over when he retired, she did enjoy helping out
occasionally when he was short-staffed.

That was what she was doing when she had met
Slade for the first time. She had been standing in for
one of their receptionists when he had walked in with
his mother, and, in the temporary absence of the head
waiter, she had shown them to their table.

Lee had never forgotten her first impression of him,
yet it hadn't been one she liked. He had been tall and
dark and too overpowering. She had resented the way
his eyes had glittered over her slight figure, her long
graceful neck and beautiful little head. He had asked
abruptly who she was.

When she had reluctantly revealed her identity, his
mother had insisted that she sat with them for a few

minutes. Apparently Mrs Western had known her
mother, and she had talked to Lee sympathetically
while her black-browed son had looked on, his cool
green eyes seldom leaving Lee's face.

Lee had picked up enough sophistication in Los
Angeles to be able to hide the rather startling awareness
she felt for him. She even agreed, after refusing to join
his mother and him for dinner, to have a drink with
him later, while his mother had coffee in the lounge.
But although the Westerns were acquainted with her
family, she had no intention of having anything more to
do with him.

Slade Western, however, had other ideas. He soon
made no secret of the fact that Lee attracted him, and,
contrarily, because he possessed the mysterious ability
to make her heart race uncomfortably fast, the more he
pursued her, the more she had flirted with other men.
She didn't realise she was playing with fire until she
allowed herself to be persuaded to go to London with
his mother.

Before this she had visited his magnificent home
along the river several times, though she only accepted
invitations from Mrs Western. She enjoyed the parties
Mrs Western gave and, if she could avoid Slade, found
nothing to complain about. If she did find herself alone
with him she was careful to keep her distance.
Instinctively she had guessed she was too young to be
able to cope with a man of Slade's calibre, and she
confined herself to idle flirtations. It wasn't until weeks
later that she discovered painfully that Slade had
believed her dates with other men to be far from
innocent.

On her bed, Lee stirred restlessly, wishing she hadn't
thought of that. Living with her grandfather had
eventually began to pall. She was fond of him, but
found the country boring. When Mrs Western
suggested she should accompany her to London and
combine a holiday with being her part-time secretary,

she hadn't been able to resist. Her mother, who had always lived above her income, hadn't left any money, and while Lee had never resented this, she realised she might not have the means to visit London on her own for a long time.

Once in the capital she really began having a good time. At first she had thought Slade might have had something to do with her being there, but he had soon disabused her of that notion when he had caught her, one evening, in the arms of one of his friends. The man had actually grabbed her and kissed her against her will, but Slade, when he had got rid of him, refused to believe this. He had been furious.

'I told Lydia,'—his mother—'what would happen if she brought you here. She should have left you at River Bend. You can't resist flirting with any man who spares you a second glance, can you?'

Lee had refused to defend herself against such an outrageous attack, but she had been indignant when he went on to imply that she was just out for what she could get.

'I do help your mother, Slade, and I've every intention of finding myself a proper job soon. If I can't find one I'll go back to my grandfather.'

'You don't have to work,' he had said thickly, his eyes suddenly hot with desire. 'Live with me.'

Even if he had offered marriage she would have refused, though she might not have done so afterwards. Instead she had felt highly insulted and told him she wouldn't live with him if he was the last person on earth. But only a few days later she had been forced, through no fault of her own, at least no deliberate fault of her own, to change her mind.

Mrs Western was not a very demanding employer, and Lee's duties were far from arduous. Mostly they consisted of writing letters and making phone calls accepting and issuing invitations and making appointments. And acting in a kind of liaison capacity between

Mrs Western and her cook–housekeeper. Her mother's housekeeper had been strict, but though Lee had always rebelled against authority, they had been good friends. A month was amply long enough for someone of Lee's outgoing nature to get to know Ann Bowie well. She was a nice woman and Lee felt sorry for her.

Ann, middle-aged, had worked for the Westerns for fifteen years. She had a twenty-year-old son and no husband. Slade, Lee soon discovered, had no time for Ray Bowie, who had been in scrapes with the police ever since he left school. The last time he had threatened to ban him from the house. Ann could go too, Lee had overheard Slade telling his mother, if there was any more trouble.

Ann had told Lee a little about her past, but she made no secret of the fact that Mrs Western had taken her in when Ray was only five and this house was the only real home she had ever known. Lee was aware that she worried a lot over Ray, who was wild rather than bad and lived with friends in another part of the city. Unfortunately he was unemployed and always short of money. His mother helped him all she could, delving deeply, Lee suspected, into her savings, but he was forever in the house, complaining that he couldn't manage.

Lee believed the situation would resolve itself in time, but suddenly, to her horror, the whole thing had reached a terrifying climax, exploding devastatingly in her own face with repercussions which were to haunt her for years.

# CHAPTER THREE

IT happened one evening when Mrs Western sent her to the kitchen with a message for Ann. Lee found Ray there with his mother. The daily help had gone, as dinner was over, but Ann didn't seem too happy. She had obviously been lecturing Ray about something, because his usually care-free face was sullen and angry.

'It's okay, Mom,' Lee heard him muttering, 'haven't I just told you? I know I'm not welcome here any more and I won't be back.'

He had his hands stuck in the pockets of the old jacket he was wearing and he jerked one out impatiently to deal with a lock of hair that refused to stay out of his eyes. To the dismay of both women, as he did so, a diamond necklace came out of his pocket with it, caught on a button on his sleeve.

While Ann gasped and collapsed, looking ready to faint, Lee's eyes widened in stunned dismay. 'Wherever did you get that, Ray?' she had gasped.

'It—it belongs to Mrs Western!' Ann whispered before he could reply. 'Oh, Ray,' her worn face crumpled, 'how could you? That's what you must have been doing when you were supposed to be in my room!'

'She won't miss it,' he retorted defiantly, though Lee saw he had gone very pale. 'She has loads of the stuff,' he added, thrusting the necklace in his pocket again.

'Don't do that! Give it to me,' Ann, shaking and sobbing, was suddenly at his side, taking it from him. 'You must be mad!' she cried. 'Madam might be prepared to forgive you, but I happen to know that if Mr Slade discovers what you've done, he won't hesitate to send us both packing!'

They seemed to have forgotten Lee was there and she

41

gazed from one to the other apprehensively, trying to find something to say. 'Why did you take it, Ray?' she asked at last.

He shot her another sullen glance, but she could see he was beginning to shake as badly as his mother. 'I only wanted a bit of extra cash,' he swallowed hard. 'You don't know what it's like existing on next to nothing every day.'

'I can guess,' she said gently, realising, from the state he was in, that she didn't have to emphasise the seriousness of the situation. 'But this is no way to solve your problems. You'll have to put it back.'

'Yes,' gasped Ann, tears running pathetically down her cheeks as she agreed with Lee. 'Madam will know immediately if something is missing. You'll have to return it straight away, but you'll have to be careful.'

'I can't go back up there, Mom,' he muttered, clearly very frightened. 'I'd never make it a second time.'

Lee had seen the terrible despair on their faces. They looked like two people facing a firing squad or a future without hope. And that they appeared to trust her completely might also have had something to do with the impulsive offer she'd made. 'Look, Ann,' she had said quickly, without really pausing to think, 'give the necklace to me. I can pretend I'm going to my room. It will only take a minute to step into Mrs Western's and replace it in her jewel case. I know exactly where she keeps it, and Slade's in the study.'

He had been, but unfortunately he had caught her with the necklace in her hands, just as she had been about to put it back. Because she had known where it was kept, having helped Mrs Western to unfasten some of the difficult catches on her jewellery before, she hadn't put on the light, and she realised she must have looked the picture of guilt.

Slade hadn't given her a chance to think up an excuse. If she refused again to live with him, he would ring the police immediately and tell them he had caught her stealing.

Lee had been in a quandary and panicked before Slade's relentless expression. It had been impossible to defend herself without betraying Ray and his mother, and this she hadn't been able to bring herself to do. As the memory of Ray's frightened young face and Ann's distraught one flashed through her mind, she had known she was trapped. If she had been the only one involved she might have challenged Slade to do his worst, but, apart from Ray and Ann, there was her grandfather to consider and she dared not risk it. If Slade did send her to prison he might never get over the disgrace. So, because she seemed to have no other option and his threats seemed genuine, she felt forced to do as Slade asked.

An hour later Lee left, supposedly in answer to an urgent call from her mother's solicitors in New York. Slade had arranged everything and flown with her. He had given her no chance to escape him this time, nor had he ever stopped believing she was a thief.

The next two days Lee was convinced were the longest she had ever spent at River Bend, but when Slade didn't turn up she suspected, as she had done in the beginning, that he had merely been amusing himself and that her fears regarding him were groundless.

Julia and Nigel left on Friday, after a hustle of last-minute arrangements, and Sandra went off as well to attend a family wedding in the North. It hadn't been realised that all three would be away at the same time, but Lee scoffed at their concern over leaving her on her own.

'How do you suppose I managed before you came?' she laughed. 'You can't possibly cancel your arrangements because of me, and I certainly have no intention of coming with you.'

She did, though, think of tossing a few things in a

bag and going off to London for a few days, as a certain nervousness overtook her as she contemplated the empty drive. It had taken a lot of willpower not to ask Nigel if he knew where Slade was. She had managed to restrain her rising panic, knowing how ridiculous she was being.

The house was quiet after the others had gone, which made her conscious of the rising wind. It howled about the old roof, making it creak, and puffed in the chimneys, bringing down soot. Outside it blew through the dry, withering grass, but did nothing to disperse the shadows gathering on the tree-shaded lawns. Lee was aware of a feeling of loneliness and hoped Matt would call. He had given her a ring after lunch, but she had forgotten to ask what his plans were.

After lighting a fire, trying to keep a recurrent depression at bay, she was thinking of making some coffee when the doorbell rang. Her spirits lightened; that would be Matt. Though the door wasn't locked he didn't usually just walk in, and she hurried to open it. All her panic returned when she saw it wasn't Matt who stood there staring at her but Slade Western.

Lee found herself blushing deeply as he made no immediate attempt to either move or speak. His arms were folded over the solid breadth of his chest, his eyes hooded so she couldn't tell what he was thinking as they slid slowly down the length of her body. Drawing a quick breath as his glance seemed to lance into her, she wished he would stop looking at her like this each time they met. She wished she had worn something other than a thin summer dress and little else. Long before his gaze returned to her face she was trembling.

As he made no attempt to break the taut silence between them, she forced herself to speak. 'What do you want?' she asked abruptly.

'What a welcome for an old—friend!' he muttered, his dark eyes gleaming with either laughter or anger, she couldn't quite make out which.

She was aware of the familiar acceleration of her pulses and an accompanying despair that he could still arouse a multitude of emotions merely by looking at her. 'Even old friends aren't always welcome,' she replied evenly, refusing to be provoked. 'I was just going to have some supper.'

'Then ask me to join you,' he commanded arrogantly, daring her not to. 'Have you forgotten everything I taught you?'

Reluctantly she moved aside to let him in. 'You didn't have to teach me manners!' she flared as he closed the door she had longed to slam in his face. She frowned. He ought to know some situations were beyond ordinary politeness. 'I hope you don't intend staying long,' she said shortly, 'I have things to see to and I'm expecting Matt.'

'Matt's busy,' he copied her coldness. 'He won't be here tonight.'

'How do you know that?' she asked, bewildered.

'I've seen to it,' he replied calmly. 'We have things to talk about, you and I, and I've no wish to be interrupted.'

Lee gazed at him, incensed at his presumption. 'I can't agree that we've anything to talk about,' she returned icily, then spoiled the effect of her displeasure by adding, 'If you thought we had, you took your time coming back.'

'I had to go to London,' his smile held a hint of satisfaction as he recognised the unconscious indignation in her voice. 'And from there to Paris. Remember Paris?' he taunted softly.

She would have given almost everything she had not to. Her face went white. Paris had been magic, yet pain. It had been there that their feelings for each other had heightened unbearably, so much so that it had thrown all her other emotions into similar perspective. Every time they had explored the old courtyards, wandered down alleyways and around the Grands Boulevards, gone to concerts and danced together, the tension between them and inside her had increased until she couldn't bear it any longer. And all the while Slade had watched her without saying anything. How could he remind her of Paris when she had striven so hard to forget!

Realising they were simply standing staring at each other, Lee forced an indifferent shrug. 'If you must stay, shall we go into the lounge?' she suggested.

'You're being sensible at last,' he said smoothly, but, before she lowered eyes far too reluctant to leave him, she noticed that somehow she had managed to make him angry again.

He glanced around as she poured him a drink. The lounge was a large room, most of the furniture and paintings had belonged to Lee's grandfather and, because there was nothing in it she disliked, she had left it almost exactly as it had been in his lifetime. She had had it redecorated, which had made a difference, but that was all.

As she handed Slade his whisky and sat down, she felt his eyes following her. 'So—you've recovered from your tumble in the ditch?' he enquired, raising his glass.

'Quite!' she snapped, ignoring his silent toast and putting her own glass aside without touching it. 'I wasn't actually hurt.'

'Neither was your young friend.'

'How do you know?' She was puzzled that he should sound so sure.

'I rang,' he enlightened her. 'The boy's mother thought it kind of me.'

Lee glanced at him sharply, only to find his narrowed glance fixed on her breasts. Her breath caught and she went hot all over, and, as this betrayal of her body upset her, she desperately recovered her sherry and took a fortifying gulp. How dared he? her mind screamed, while her voice said coolly, 'She would appreciate it.'

'I thought you would think so,' he murmured, the

green of his eyes glittering slightly as he studied her a moment longer before returning his attention to the room. 'So you came back to live here? I never thought you would.'

'I——' she had been about to say she had had nowhere else to go, then decided not to. The less Slade knew of her hopes and fears concerning that period of her life the better. She wondered if he had known of her accident but she doubted it and wasn't going to tell him. 'My grandfather wanted me to live here.'

'After you settled down?'

She refused to rise to his taunt. 'It happens to suit me.'

'Better than Paris, Rome, New York?'

She looked at him quickly as he threw back his whisky and his glass hit the mantelshelf sharply. In all those places she had been the mistress of a man whose business and financial genius was both feared and respected. She might have been a pawn in his high-powered life, but, whatever Slade's faults, he had protected her almost fanatically from the seamier aspects of such a position. If a word against her had got back to him the person who uttered it had lived to rue the day.

'Don't say you didn't enjoy those months,' he jeered when she didn't reply.

She sat rigid on the sofa, her lower lip sore from where she had been biting it. 'I can't deny that,' she admitted jerkily, for in truth it had been an exciting time, and her growing love for Slade had eased the trauma of its rougher passages, even if it had made other things unbearable.

'You enjoyed what I could give you,' he said harshly, as though he wasn't merely making a statement but seeking answers to things that had long puzzled him.

'Yes,' Lee admitted again, 'but I've changed, Slade. I don't place such importance on valueless things any more.'

That appeared to catch him on the raw, and for a moment he looked almost savage. 'Indeed!' he retorted, a dull flush under his taut skin. 'I don't see any great evidence of a change, so far. You're still careless to the point of being criminally reckless, and your appearance hasn't altered any. You could still be nineteen.'

Her cheeks paled at the cruelty of his attack, which seemed to go beyond mere words. But he had never been interested in sparing her feelings, and she wondered why he had ever bothered, in the past, to shield her from other people. He had only been interested in one thing. Yet sometimes they had talked. Sometimes they had lingered for hours over a cup of coffee, finding themselves capable of communicating with each other on a level which had, if anything, enhanced their physical relationship.

She sighed unhappily. He still clung to the opinion he had formed of her years ago. Arguing with him wouldn't alter it. 'I'm tired, Slade,' she replied tautly. 'It's getting late.'

'Once you didn't mind how late it was,' he reminded her grimly.

Again she sighed. 'If you're going to turn everything I say into an excuse to rake up the past . . .'

'May I sit down?' he broke in abruptly.

'If you must.'

He lowered his long length into what she had began to think of as Matt's chair, and she had to grit her teeth to hide her resentment. Slade reacted to any kind of opposition like a challenge and didn't miss a thing.

'Did your grandfather leave you much money?' he asked conversationally, 'The house looks well, if not in the peak of condition.'

Of course he would notice the shabbiness! His own properties were immaculate and he never stinted on luxurious appointments. 'A lot of us can't afford the best,' she said coldly. 'Grandfather left me River Bend but no money.'

He considered her thoughtfully with those green eyes that could so easily turn black. 'You could have sold it, yet you're still here. Why, when you used to find it so dull?'

There he was, going back again, and she didn't want to talk about that. She hadn't found living here dull, not ever. She had merely been young and restless. 'I have three—well, I suppose you could call them lodgers. Two agency nurses and a man. Nigel Blakey, incidentally, works for you. I thought the house would be too big for me on my own,' she explained, not sure why she bothered, 'And they're good company.'

He didn't seem too surprised, and she wondered just how much he had gleaned from Matt. 'Where are they now?' he asked deviously.

She hated having to tell him. 'Julia and Nigel are on holiday together while Sandra has gone home for a family wedding.'

'Love makes the world go round,' he drawled sarcastically.

'What's wrong with that?' she snapped, staring at his hard dark face and sensuous mouth, willing herself not to feel wounded.

'Nothing, if you're gullible enough,' he retorted, then more softly, 'Aren't you nervous about spending the night here alone?'

Her blue eyes were mutinous. 'I've plenty to keep me occupied. I won't have time to think of it.'

'Ah, yes,' his eyes glinted mockingly. 'I've heard you write. Successfully?'

'If that's supposed to be a question,' she replied, an edge on her voice for he sounded disparaging, 'the answer is yes, occasionally. I'll never make a fortune, but I earn enough to keep the wolf from the door. Some of them,' she added pointedly.

His mouth twisted at her sharp dig, otherwise he ignored it. 'You illustrate your own books?'

He looked interested, but Lee sensed there was more

behind his apparently innocent queries than that. 'So
far,' she said tersely. 'But that's because, until now,
what I've done hasn't called for anything elaborate.'

'And now?' he prompted.

'Now my publisher thinks my books deserve the help
of a proper illustrator,' she shrugged, 'but I don't
know . . .' Why am I telling Slade all this? she wondered disconcertingly. Why don't I just tell him to get
lost and concentrate on what's important in my life,
such as settling down and marrying Matt?

His eyes narrowed on her disturbed face. 'You always
craved excitement, you seldom relaxed. Everything you
did was at twice the normal pace. You could almost
exhaust me, and I'm not unrenowned for my staying
powers. I'm finding it difficult to associate the girl I
knew then with the one you pretend to be now. The
high-spirited girl who was never too tired to go
anywhere, do anything, would have found it impossible
to settle for the usually isolated life of a writer.'

Lee went white. Didn't he understand that the furious
pace he accused her of setting had been prompted more
by her feelings of humility and insecurity than anything
else? Yet, if he hadn't understood, had it been entirely
his fault? Confused, Lee halted her tumultuous
thoughts to think about it. Would she have let Slade
believe she was a thief, even for the sake of Ann and
Ray, if she hadn't been attracted to him? She began to
wonder if she hadn't unconsciously taken advantage of
the situation to give herself an excuse for surrendering
to him. In the beginning she had been too filled with a
sense of excitement, curiosity and the startling discovery
of her own sensuality to question if she was doing the
right thing. Slade was a brilliant and powerful man,
possessed of something far beyond mere good looks. He
could dwarf other men of equal stature. He was wealthy
and could give her almost anything she wanted. Too
late she had realised that the two things she had really
wanted were his love and marriage, but he never

mentioned either of them. And, after six months, the knowledge that she would never be more than his mistress was something she had found impossible to come to terms with.

'I like writing,' she said, confused by such an invasion of unwelcome thoughts. 'I really have changed.'

'Not too much, I hope?'

Lee felt colour creeping under her skin as the near-insolence in his voice taunted her. Remember Matt, she kept on telling herself, don't take any notice of Slade. He has an evil knack of slamming the past in one's face with every seemingly innocuous sentence. He didn't have to come right out with anything. Every glance more than hinted that he had forgotten nothing and that somewhere behind that urbane façade some kind of fire, composed of she knew not what, still smouldered, refusing to go out.

She made a determined effort to keep the conversation impersonal. 'I think I've been fortunate in finding something to do that I like.'

'Once you liked the way I could make you feel.'

Unwisely she retorted, 'That was sex.'

'I'm glad you admit it.'

How nice it would be to slap that sardonic smile off his face! 'I wasn't doing it for a living!' she choked.

'Weren't you?'

How she hated him! With Slade she had lived a life of luxury, she couldn't deny it, and he had showered her with presents of every kind. How thankful she was that when she had left him she had left everything behind. She was suddenly curious as to his feelings after she had flown. She had wondered a lot of times, but never before had she felt so urgently in need to know, yet something fleeting in his eyes warned her not to ask. There was a rawness about him that suggested incredibly that some residue of the emotions he had experienced then were still there—whatever they had been?

'You gave me no opportunity to look for a job,' she said defensively.

'Or even to think of one,' his eyes darkened softly. 'Didn't you ever wonder why I spared you so much time?'

Lee frowned, not wishing to dwell on it. He was delighting in her discomfiture—to discuss the past with him could be disastrous. To remember the hold he had had over her should be warning enough. She stirred restlessly, too conscious of his virile figure and something in his eyes that she couldn't believe was the same expression that had once warned her of his stirring desire. Unexpectedly her heart-rate increased dramatically and she jumped to her feet, just managing to suppress a frightened shudder.

She didn't answer his question, but he didn't appear to notice. In a flash he was on his own feet and forcing her down on the sofa again. This time he sat beside her. He used little strength, but her traitorous limbs seemed bent on obeying him against her will. His hand was on her arm, the warmth of his breath on her cheek, and, as she felt the muscles of his powerful thighs pressing against hers, her heart took off on another burst of speed. When she accused him in a strangled voice of using brute force to get his own way, he laughed lazily and looked not the least bit repentant.

'I really have things to do, Slade,' she snapped, not caring for the gleam of determination in his eyes. 'I don't want to talk.'

'Neither do I.' His voice roughened as he held her firmly, then quickly slipped an arm around her to draw her ruthlessly closer. Before she could move, she was crushed to the hardness of his body and felt the heat of him searing her, even through her clothes. 'I have no intention of leaving,' he muttered.

'Matt!' she cried, as if hoping his name might drive a wedge between them.

'I've already told you, I've given him so much to do he won't be here tonight.'

Lee's lips went dry, her throat closing in panic. Slade was holding her tightly and his sexuality was so potent that it quickened her blood, making her helpless to fight it. His hands caressed her slowly, generating sparks of electricity wherever they touched. He didn't seem to have forgotten a thing about her and was obviously taking advantage of his previous knowledge of her to gain his own ends!

'You're giving Matt work deliberately,' she accused, miserably, 'in order to split us up.'

He eased back slightly to gaze down at her, a certain possessiveness in his eyes that she didn't understand. The coldness had gone, but what remained seemed an even greater threat than his former anger.

'I'm doing the only possible thing,' he retorted. 'Given a little sensible guidance, Matt will soon find someone else.'

'You don't think I'm good enough!' she flared, sudden fury enabling her to escape him and stumble to her feet.

To her surprise he let her go this time. 'I don't think you are,' he agreed brutally. 'And you're getting out of his life.'

Furiously she lashed back, 'You have no hold over me! No right to try and tell me what to do!'

'Haven't I?' he drawled. 'I think you're mistaken. We had an agreement, you and I, and you didn't keep your side of it. You promised me two years.'

Oh, God, he wasn't going to start on about that! 'Slade, that's all part of the past,' she tried to reason, then faltered again before she could find the strength to continue. 'You may feel you have a legitimate complaint, but you can't possibly want me now. Besides, I've rebuilt my whole life. I'm engaged and intend to marry. You have no right to come back and spoil everything for me again!'

Slowly he got up and moved towards her, as if it was imperative to keep her under close surveillance. With his eyes fixed on her, he replied tightly, 'A lot of what happened you brought on yourself and it was a mistake to opt out of your side of the bargain. A thief shouldn't really consider he has any rights at all, and to get involved with one of my relations was chancing your luck just a bit too far.'

'Matt could hardly be called a relation!' she retorted hotly.

'Maybe not a close one,' he conceded, 'but I did warn you.'

'I thought you meant just to stay away from your mother.'

'Then you're wrong.'

'Slade,' she implored, suddenly hating that he should think so badly of her, 'I love Matt.'

'You don't,' he said grimly. 'You aren't capable of loving any man.'

'Matt doesn't believe that.'

'More fool him!' Slade glared at her, increasing the pain in her heart.

'I'm not a thief,' she whispered impulsively. 'I know it looked that way . . .'

He laughed harshly. 'Don't you think you've left it rather late to try and convince me? I caught you at it, remember? Pretty damning evidence, wouldn't you say?'

'Things aren't always as they look.'

His mouth curled derisively. 'You've had time to think. It might be interesting to hear how you intend absolving yourself?'

When it came to it, she couldn't. For all she knew Ann Bowie might still be working for his mother. Too late she wished she hadn't said anything; it had only made matters worse. 'I'm sorry, I can't,' she faltered miserably. 'But I have changed.'

'Changed?' he mocked, his glance sweeping over her. 'I don't think so, not even in appearance. You're still beautiful and sexy enough to stop a man in his tracks. And still capable of deceiving.'

Lee's cheeks flooded with hot colour as she retorted fiercely, 'I can't convince you, can I?'

'Perhaps I should convince you,' he muttered thickly, his arms reaching out to enfold her again.

She wanted to run, but again the mere touch of him had her limbs reduced to water. He was using his old ability to control her quite blatantly. The most she could do was to try and annihilate him with blazing eyes.

Her temper appeared only to amuse him, and, as his bold dark gaze bored into her, a feeling of peculiar lightness began enveloping her whole body. Crazily, she felt she was floating in an entirely new dimension, thirsting for something she had been denied for too long.

As he loomed above her, dwarfing her slight five foot five, she began to tremble while her eyes clung to him helplessly. She regarded him hungrily. His hair was still thick and dark, his features as relentlessly moulded. Only his sensuous mouth betrayed the warmth and vitality of that side of his nature that had been able to turn her to wax in his arms. She became aware that he was staring at her as intently as she was staring at him, and, as his eyes darkened, as the chemistry between them renewed itself with frightening force, all the fight went out of her, leaving her completely defenceless.

Her face burning, she lowered her eyes for fear he might read the feelings of longing and need stabbing through her. She knew despair that he could still affect her like this, to stir her senses to such a dangerous pitch in a way no other man, not even Matt, had been able to.

'Look at me!' commanded Slade in a low voice.

Shock reverberated through her whole being as she weakly obeyed and saw the total self-assurance in his eyes. With a faint smile he slid cool fingers down her feverish cheeks, a habit of his, she recalled, and was sure he was doing it deliberately to remind her. It was

an intentional provocation—as though she wasn't
disturbed enough!—to rouse the masses of electricity
that he could evoke with the ease of pressing a switch.

She realised she should be fighting him but could
only gaze at him blindly as his fingers traced the outline
of her taut lips, then moved more swiftly along her jaw,
through the thickness of her silky hair to capture the
slender curve of her nape. His hand was gentle, yet she
was intensely aware of the steel in its grip. A
ruthlessness existed under the cloaking tolerance of his
manner which she attempted to view with wariness but
failed. How could she keep her thoughts fixed on all the
devilish things she should remember about him when he
was rapidly rendering her mindless?

When he lowered his mouth to tantalisingly explore
the cheek his fingers had just caressed, instinctively she
turned her head to accommodate his teasing lips. His
continuing restraint, which she didn't know hid a desire
to crush to the point of violence, inflamed her almost
beyond endurance. She found it impossible to hide her
response from him. In any case, the pounding of her
heart under the thinness of her dress would have given
her away. Wordlessly she remained clenched against
him, only able to whisper his name.

As something in her tone revealed the extent of the
hunger consuming her, his mouth found hers ruthlessly,
with a demanding heat that in seconds had her weak
and yielding, her hands clutching in his hair. It was
earth-shaking. His kiss deepened to a hot, drugging
sweetness that emptied her head of everything but a
growing physical need. A wild recklessness filled her,
sweeping aside the years since Slade had kissed her like
this, with the force of a tidal wave. He didn't hurry, he
knew just how much she could take before her
resistance broke, but she was too carried away to care.
He had her head tilted back to the command of his
hand, and as his mouth explored every inch of her
throat, soft broken moans escaped her bruised lips.

Lee felt her body melting bonelessly against him as he drifted his lips back across her face. She sensed that his caresses were deliberately prolonged, a careful seduction, but though her mind was still trying to warn her, she craved what he was doing to her. Dazedly she admitted she had never been able to resist.

Her hands were suddenly working frenziedly on his shirt, slipping it from under the waistband of his trousers. Too impatient to bother with buttons, she was acting like someone drunk, but with an unerring grasp of going after what she wanted. Slade helped her when once her fingers fumbled, he even guided her so she could rediscover the breadth of his chest. The mat of hair she found there made her palms tingle and she drew a sharp breath. She hadn't known how deprived she had been, or realised the devastating bleakness of her life until he was holding her like this.

Slade's own ragged breathing seemed to indicate that he was no less affected by the storm of desire sweeping through them than she was. Feeling that this implied that at least some of her attraction for him hadn't died, her heart began racing so fast she wondered if he could hear it? As his mouth invaded hers, then trailed another deluge of burning kisses over her face and neck, he aroused in her a sweet, aching torment that only he could satisfy. Need of him rippled through her like a burning tide, causing her arms to slide round his back to press him urgently closer.

His mouth was hard and hot and she shuddered, responding to his passion, matching it with her own. There was something primitive in the kisses they exchanged, the way he held her, but if she whimpered with unconscious pain he didn't hear her but went on kissing her like a man deprived.

Every bit of Lee came alive as sensation electrified every part of her body. It had been over five years, and during those years she had come to believe that such a capacity for feeling had been left behind with her teens.

She recalled emotions so intense she had been apprehensive of them, even ashamed. If she had been Slade's wife she could have lived with the wild wantonness he had filled her with every time he made love to her, but because she was only his mistress she had began to feel that such feelings should be suppressed. Yet within a few minutes of being in his arms once more, here she was, longing frantically to belong to him again.

When the telephone rang she heard herself begging him, in a voice she didn't recognise, not to answer it. She willed him not to answer it, being doubtful, if he left her now, that she would ever survive.

He muttered against her mouth, 'I've been a fool to stay away as long.' To her surprise his voice shook, though he controlled it as the ringing continued. 'You'd better answer it. If it's Matt, it could be for me.'

Stumbling from him, Lee picked up the receiver, only half aware of the implications of what he had said. It was Matt. 'Matt!' she exclaimed hoarsely. 'I—where are you? I thought you were busy.'

'I have to speak to Slade,' he said slowly, as if he recognised her confused state, even over the phone, and was disturbed by it.

'Sl—Slade?' she stammered.

'Are you all right, Lee?' Matt asked sharply, but before she could reply the receiver was taken from her hand. 'She's fine, Matt,' Slade said curtly. 'We're just talking over old times.'

# CHAPTER FOUR

As Lee tried to find her voice through the anger that flooded her as Slade spoke, she became aware, from Slade's monosyllabic replies, that Matt was relaying some information he must have asked for. There was a brief pause, then Slade said smoothly, 'That's all I wanted to know. I'll see you tomorrow.'

He replaced the receiver without even having the decency to hand it back to her, but she was too incensed to notice. 'Why did you tell him you would be here?' she accused.

'Why should I not?' Slade countered coolly. 'It was important that he knew where to reach me.'

'You mustn't stay any longer,' she breathed, her anger turning to misery. 'He sounded suspicious.'

There was a long, pregnant silence, then he drew her into his arms again. 'Does it matter?' he asked, playing idly with a strand of her luxuriant long hair, Matt clearly already out of his mind.

'It does to me,' she replied, yet her voice lacked conviction. 'He won't know what to think.'

Slade lifted his broad shoulders indifferently. 'Maybe it will help to prepare him for the moment when you tell him you're through.'

'Never!'

'That's a long time,' he said dryly, covering her indignant mouth with his.

She tried to push him away, but could only offer half-hearted resistance to his sensual expertise. The subtle pressure of his kiss sent all aggression fleeing and, as her lips parted under the provocative insistence of his, she sagged against him weakly. In a daze, she heard him murmuring, 'What's mine I never give up, Lee. And don't pretend you don't still want me as much as I want you.'

She would have denied it if she had been able to hide the truth. Not only her body but her mind was on fire for him—there was no other way to describe the overwhelming force of the desire which flamed through every bit of her to the exclusion of everything else.

As Slade sensed her surrender some of his forcefulness faded. When he lifted her chin so he could look at her, his hand was gentle. 'Do you remember the first time we made love?' he asked thickly. 'It's a night I haven't been able to forget.'

'Nor me,' she whispered fervently, blue eyes darkening, as memories flooded back.

'I've tried to forget,' he groaned. 'Until I heard of your engagement, I thought I'd succeeded.'

Lee winced as his mouth twisted wryly, but she didn't move. His faint amusement, however, drove her to taunt, 'Haven't other women helped?'

'No!' His humour, which she didn't know had been more a form of self-mockery, disappeared. 'Other women—or men—don't come into this. I want you, and there won't be any more running away this time. There won't be any escape.'

'I managed to before.'

Anger flickered briefly through his eyes. 'That was because I didn't believe it possible that you could turn your back on what we had.'

'Slade!' she implied, wanting to be reminded of anything but that! 'If you don't care about mine, won't you at least consider Matt's feelings?'

'No!' he retorted furiously.

She gulped at the unguarded violence in his face. 'But . . .'

Placing swift fingers over her lips, he stemmed further words. 'Matt's feelings will soon sort themselves out. Forget him.'

'I can't.' But she was speaking mechanically,

protesting merely because she thought she should be, only a tiny part of her sincerely defending her commitment to Matt. Yet she gasped with near shock as Slade's lips descended again abruptly and struggled fiercely as the harshness of his kiss blotted Matt out completely. Her pulse leapt as Slade's plundering mouth ruthlessly removed her ability to think of anyone but him. Eyes closed, she trembled in his arms as he pushed his hot face into her neck, his mouth moving on her burning skin.

The years since they had last met might never have been, but there was a new element in his embrace that she sensed rather than understood. He no longer seemed to have the almost inhuman ability to control the strength of his feelings. She felt his heart pounding into her, almost hurting her with the intensity of its violent beat. His breathing was audible and uneven as he pressed hot lips to the pulsing perimeter of her throat. His passion consumed her until she felt as weak and helpless as a kitten, and he kept on kissing her until her legs threatened to withdraw their support.

Never before could she remember Slade making love to her quite like this, as if his emotions had moved on to a new and frightening plane. There was a wildness in him that suggested she had managed to unlock a door previously kept tightly closed and something rawly elemental was pouring through it out of him. Whatever it was she wasn't sure, but she found herself responding to it with a fierce exultation she made no attempt to hide. She felt an aching sensation flooding her lower limbs and was suddenly clinging to him, silently abandoning herself to the terrible driving urgency that had them both in its grip.

She wasn't really conscious of him removing their clothes with hands uncharacteristically unsteady. As desire mounted crazily inside her everything else was blotted from her mind. When he lifted her and laid her gently down on the thick rug in front of the fire, the hardness of the floor made little impression until he lowered himself on top of her. Even then she made no demur but arched herself blindly against him. Feeling the roughness of his chest scratching the softness of her breasts, she shivered with pleasure rather than pain. She heard the intake of his breath as their mouths met and clung, and the violence of their bodies meeting in searing impact made what they had known before seem like a milk-and-water thing by comparison.

Swiftly he parted her legs, not trying to hide his complete arousal. Other times he had enjoyed making slow love to her, making her wait when she had often begged him to take her, but now it seemed as if a dam had burst, sweeping everything before it, and with it the time or need for any preliminaries. Hot and breathless, Lee gasped, half crazed as he joined them almost savagely together, and her small tortured cry brought barely a pause to the thrusting hardness of his possession. Then, as passion spilled over them, consuming them, lifting them to a world completely removed from the one they were in, he brought her once more to that shuddering, ecstatic peak of delight that she had almost forgotten existed.

They lay in front of the fire together, but they could have been anywhere. They shared the aftermath of passion with the same sensitivity that had once held them so closely together. Lee trembled slightly and Slade made no attempt to leave her, and while she was happy that it should be so, she wished she could have avoided his searching eyes.

'I hurt you,' he frowned. 'I know I was impatient, but surely there've been others since me?'

'There's been no one,' she confessed raggedly, her hands slowly clenching, as the admission seemed torn from her.

'Why not?' he asked huskily, his eyes still boring into her. 'It's been a long time.'

It was a question she couldn't answer, for even before Matt men had never stopped issuing invitations which she had declined. It was something she had often wondered about herself—only now, in Slade's arms, did she suddenly know why. 'I couldn't—with another man,' she admitted, not sure she was being wise. Wasn't she vulnerable enough without Slade knowing this about her?

He kissed her softly, his mouth very gentle. 'Lee, my darling, the time we've wasted; the years we might have shared!'

'I don't know . . .' she whispered uncertainly, while wondering if he could be right. Her fingers wound through his hair and she was startled by the way his magnificent body trembled when she touched him, yet she could feel his stomach muscles clenching as if he was trying to hide it from her.

'It's been too long,' he said thickly, and she quivered as if a chill wind had suddenly touched her.

'Yes,' she agreed dully. The shock of her accident, the subsequent loss of memory had dulled the edge of her passion for him, helping her to stop rushing back to him as she had been tempted to do on her flight from Paris, when her body had been tormented with raw need for the man she had been fleeing from. The anguish it had aroused had made her careless and the car had knocked her down, and though she had recovered her memory, the six months she had spent with Slade had remained blurred.

The remark of a doctor came back to her. 'Some things you might not remember because you don't want to,' he had warned. She realised that the exact degree of her involvement with Slade might have been the kind of thing he was referring to. Yet now that she experienced full recall, she couldn't help feeling apprehensive of it. There was no doubting Slade's renewed ardency, but did the future hold anything more for her now than it had done before?

'Could you marry Matt now?' asked Slade, the confidence in his voice challenging her to say she could.

'No,' she sighed, knowing it wouldn't be possible, not after what had just taken place.

He murmured against her cheek, 'I'm glad you've decided to be sensible.'

Sensible? Her eyes were briefly troubled. Slade was devious. In some ways she had never got close to him, and there were some things on which they might never agree, but while the breaking of her engagement was unavoidable, she doubted if it could be called sensible.

'You'll tell him tomorrow?' Slade urged.

'Tomorrow?'

His eyes hardened. 'The sooner the better.'

'I suppose so,' she nodded, wishing she could spare Matt the hurt he was going to suffer but aware that there was no other course open to her.

Satisfied, Slade kissed her gently again, like a kind of reward. 'You won't regret it,' he promised magnanimously, slowly disentangling their limbs and getting to his feet.

'Where are you going?' she asked, feeling too lethargic to move. Her heartbeats increased as she watched unashamedly, as he pulled on his pants. He had a magnificent body, broad shoulders, narrow hips and powerful thighs. Something of a rumoured Continental ancestor seemed reflected in the angle of his head and the strength of his long, muscled legs. He might certainly have some Latin blood in his veins, she thought, knowing the extreme passion he was capable of.

'I want to ring my mother and tell her I won't be home tonight,' he replied, pulling up his zip. 'I only got home a few hours ago and she might be wondering where I've got to.'

'You—you won't mention you're here?' she queried uncertainly.

'No,' he shot her a cynical glance as she sat up

sharply and swiftly grabbed a rug from the sofa to cover her nakedness. 'For your sake, though, not mine.'

Lee flushed, not looking at him. 'You could go home—later.'

'Ah,' he grinned, a sudden gleam in his eye, 'so you aren't willing to part with me yet?'

Her hot cheeks grew even hotter as he picked up the phone and dialled his home number and after leaving a message returned to her. 'She gets alarmed if I just disappear. You don't mind, do you?'

She knew he occasionally used a bodyguard, but that wasn't so unusual for business men in the present decade, though it was a facility he made more use of abroad than in the U.K. 'How is your mother?' she asked, trying to believe that Mrs Western wouldn't be wondering where he was.

'Fine,' he said quietly. 'Making more fuss over my unmarried state but, on the whole, just the same.'

'You're staying a while, I hear?'

'The house needs to be lived in,' he retorted briefly, crouching by her side.

'You've never married?' She remembered his mother had always wished he would.

'No,' he smiled carelessly into her uncertain eyes. 'I'm not the marrying sort, as you well know. I've seen too many good relationships ruined by the presence of that little gold ring.'

Lee suspected the reason why Slade had never married was more complex than that, though it might simply be that he had never met the right girl. A chill went over her as she managed to reply lightly, 'If people marry for the right reasons it should have every chance of being a success.'

He continued to grin lazily, his eyes curiously blank. 'Our kind of association is the best. What we have can only improve.'

'How?'

'As if you didn't know, my beautiful darling,' he

teased, bending forward to kiss her pouting lips. 'You're even better than you used to be, and that's saying something! I'm utterly captivated. I want to stay with you—see the dawn in with you, and I've never wanted to do that with another woman.'

Lee had heard it rumoured that when he took a woman home he rarely lingered, but that didn't make her feel any happier. Unconsciously she shivered.

Feeling her tremble, Slade associated it with other things. A moment later he was guiding her upstairs. 'What you need is a hot bath.'

Would it help dispel all the shadows? Lee wished she could think straight as she walked up the wide staircase with Slade's arm protectively around her, feeling very slight and small against his superior height.

'It seems strange to find the old house so silent,' he mused, walking into the bathroom.

'I like it this way,' she replied softly. 'But it was Grandfather who closed the restaurant.'

'You had no fancy to run it?'

'No, and I didn't really have the experience.'

She had expected him to argue that she could have learned, but he merely nodded and began running taps. 'Come on,' he said, when the bath was half full, 'in you get.'

Because the bath wasn't big enough for two, he had a shower while Lee soaked, but he was soon back, lifting her out of it and carrying her through to her bedroom. With growing delight she clung to him as he lay down beside her on the soft mattress. It didn't seem to matter that they were still both wet as their eyes devoured the perfection of each other's bodies. Lee's heart beat a crazy tattoo against her ribs as, under his caressing hands, a heavy sweetness began pressing the breath from her lungs, and evidence of his renewed passion excited her immeasurably. Her hips moved instinctively and she felt the probe of his instant response against her trembling thighs.

'You're beautiful, Lee!' The softly uttered words were like explosions of pure feeling as his heart thundered against her as he captured her mouth with soul-shaking intensity. Her hand moved convulsively across the taut flesh of his stomach and she felt the trembling of his abdominal muscles. His skin was smooth over hard, vital sinews . . .

'Do you know what you're doing to me?' he muttered, an agony of frustration in his voice. 'I always wanted you before, but now I can't seem to wait.'

His kisses and murmurings had swiftly reduced her to a state beyond words and though her lips sought to form a reply nothing came out. As her tongue tasted the slightly salty skin of his neck, his mouth came down with hungry accuracy on the tautened nipple of one breast and she gasped as her own stomach muscles moved convulsively. When his hand captured her other breast, then moved slowly downwards towards another place of unbearable sensitivity, she felt a gathering storm of sensation spiral higher and higher.

A fierce trembling shook Slade's whole body as he struggled to wrest control from the primitive whirlwind that was gathering them both in its turbulent vortex. 'You're killing me!' he groaned, seconds before they were completely lost in a tempestuous rush of desire. Thunder rolled suddenly outside, rattling the windows, but the turbulence of their passion obliterated all other thought so that neither of them heard it. Lee's cries, soft at first, mounted as she was crushed beneath him, becoming more and more uninhibited. And then, like fireworks going off, a white-hot ecstasy spread through her whole body in incredible waves, just as Slade shuddered violently against her.

Much later, in bed, she turned her head to watch him sleeping. He might not love her, but he was clearly as enthralled by her as she was by him. He had left her in no doubt of this, as midnight had been long past before he had closed his eyes, and if any further evidence was needed, it could surely be found in her aching limbs.

Yet where would it all lead to? she wondered. He had come back into her life with a force she couldn't fight, in much the same way as he had entered it when she was nineteen. Her heart was sad for Matt, for the marriage they could never have, for even if she could bring herself to marry him now, wouldn't it be cheating? She felt a little sorry for herself, too, for the dreams of a husband and family she must say goodbye to. She had had her future all planned—all in vain, she thought hollowly. Slade had returned and in an incredibly short time shown her exactly how futile such a dream had been. Whether she liked it or not, she was tied to a man who would use her and cast her off when it suited him. And when that day came, she would have to endure the pain of it on her own as it would be criminal to let another man like Matt believe she might come to love him.

Wistfully, as she went on regarding Slade's sleeping form, hope rose within her. Perhaps in time he might change his mind and want to marry her? It was a fragile hope, but all she could cling to. He didn't deny the passion that held them together; if only he could learn to love her everything might be perfect. As she quietly contemplated such a soul-shaking possibility, Lee's long lashes drifted softly on to her cheeks and her mouth curved in the beginnings of a smile as she turned in Slade's enfolding arms and snuggled against him.

She woke to the sound of a lone bird chirping in the trees on the lawn and the knowledge that the storm had passed and the sun was rising. A curtain at the window flapped on a sudden current of air, then stilled, and for a moment her eyes remained blankly on it. It seemed like just another morning, until she remembered the passion-filled night and the unenviable task she had somehow to perform today.

Where was Slade? Anxiously she glanced around. The

place where he had lain was empty and there was no sign of him. Had he left already? Bitterly her soft mouth tightened. It would be just like him to disappear without a word! Always he had wanted to be acquainted with her every movement, every moment of the day, but he had hated having to give any explanation regarding any plans of his own.

Getting out of bed, she hurried to the window and when she saw his car had gone, knew her suspicions were correct. The silent house confirmed it as she pulled on a thin cotton robe and wandered listlessly downstairs to make some tea. She felt surprisingly shaky.

The phone rang as she passed through the hall and she swerved automatically to answer it. Thinking it might be Slade to apologise for his abrupt departure, her hand trembled as she picked it up. Then dismay and disappointment hit her as she realised it was Matt.

'You—you're early!' she stammered.

'Not that early!' He sounded slightly stiff and as puzzled by her confused state as he had been the night before. 'I've been trying to find Slade. He isn't at the works and his mother says he's been out all night.'

'I—well, he isn't here!' she continued stammering, though her voice strengthened as she believed she was speaking truthfully.

'I just thought he might have told you where he was going,' said Matt in lighter tones.

'Sorry,' she breathed. 'Is it something urgent?'

'Not that urgent,' he hedged. 'I'm seeing him after lunch, but I know he has other appointments this morning and it was just a point I wanted to make before he gets tied up.'

'I'm sure you'll find him somewhere.'

'Yes,' said Matt. 'It's a lovely morning.'

'Lovely!' she agreed, unable to understand the enthusiasm in her voice until she realised it was partly hysteria. Slade had told her ruthlessly to break her engagement, but somehow she couldn't. Not over the phone!

'I'll see you tonight, definitely!' Matt promised as he said goodbye.

Carefully Lee ran a finger over the receiver as she put it down, removing a speck of dust, then she nearly dropped it as she heard a noise and swung round to find Slade standing behind her. 'W-what a fright you gave me!' she gasped, face white. 'I thought you'd gone?'

'So it seems!' he snapped, his eyes resting on her icily.

For some reason he was in a rage. It mightn't be obvious to a stranger, but she knew all the signs. 'Where have you been?' she exclaimed.

'I was putting my car out of sight as you're always so careful of your reputation,' he drawled sarcastically. 'Now I think I know why.'

'Why . . .?' she repeated, staring at him blankly.

'That was Matt, wasn't it?' he rasped.

'Looking for you.'

'So,' the harsh note in his voice made her move back slightly, 'why didn't you tell him you no longer want to marry him?'

He must have been standing behind her all the time! 'How could I, over the phone?' she protested, thrusting her masses of red hair nervously off her small, pale face 'I surely owe him more consideration than that?'

Slade's sensual lips tightened to a hard, straight line before he spoke. 'Whichever way you do it couldn't be any worse than letting him go on living in a fool's paradise!'

'Give me a chance!' she cried, with a mixture of pleading and indignation. 'I didn't have time.'

'I'm sure you had,' he said furiously, his arms snaking out to draw her to him so that every inch of her fragile body was crushed against the hardness of his Then, as she whispered another protest, he begar kissing her until Matt's image faded and she began feeling faint.

Slade hadn't finished. Raising his head, he glared down on her flushed cheeks and bruised mouth. 'If you imagined I might have changed my mind about your engagement to Matt this morning, then you're wrong. You belong to me!'

Tears entered her eyes. 'I don't really belong to anyone, do I?'

He frowned a little at the bitterness in her voice. 'Not in the way most women appear to believe imperative for their pride and peace of mind, but nothing could chain us more securely together, Lee, than the ties we already have.'

'You only want my body,' she whispered, despairing at his sheer indifference as to what really mattered to her.

'It's a very beautiful body,' he teased, easing her from him slightly to allow his dark glance to slide appreciatively over her. 'I may have my faults, but you can't fault my taste.'

'Only your intentions,' she retorted sharply.

A hint of wariness flickered through his eyes. 'They've always been as honourable as you deserve. I don't think you've any reason to complain.'

'Don't you?' she replied mutinously, thinking of all she was being forced to give up.

Reading her mind, he taunted dryly, 'Come now, Lee. Is it my fault that you saw the future in terms of total unreality? As I've told you before, a husband would suit you no more than a wife would suit me.'

'And I've told you I've changed!' she snapped back, pulling herself out of his arms. 'I love Matt and did intend making him a good wife. He may not have got on in the world like you have, but at least he's got more integrity in his little finger than you have in the whole of your body. You're completely unprincipled.'

Slade's scorn turned to anger. 'If I'm unprincipled

then it's a case of the pot calling the kettle black! You can still say you love Matt after spending the night in my arms. If that's the measure of a woman's love,' he continued harshly, 'then heaven preserve me from it!'

Lee's head drooped as she turned from the derision in his eyes. Tears began streaming down her cheeks, but a thread of fury enabled her to retort, 'While I'll admit there's still something between us, you intentionally took advantage of my weakness just to gain your own ends. You came here deliberately to destroy my engagement, otherwise I would certainly never have sought you out and betrayed Matt with you.'

As she began to sob in earnest, his face darkened. 'What happened last night was inevitable, you know that, though it was never my deliberate intention to make love to you. I prefer to believe that I came to save Matt from the clutches of a woman who could never make him happy.'

'What makes you presume I couldn't make him happy?' she cried.

'Because of the way you respond to me,' he said derisively.

'You made me!' she half screamed, her voice rising as she faced him wildly. 'Even in the beginning. You blackmailed me . . .'

'Lee, for heaven's sake!'

She slapped away the calming hand he would have laid on her shoulder. 'Don't touch me!' she choked. 'I hate you. I just want you to keep away from me. I never want to see you again!'

Grinding his teeth, he brooded over her small, heaving figure. 'You won't feel like that for long. Once you come to your senses, you'll be grateful . . .'

'How dare you!' she broke in. 'I won't listen!' Fury lending wings to her feet, she glared at him as she fled upstairs. 'Just get out of here, Slade Western, and if you ever come back I'll call the police!'

She heard the front door slam with a crash that

seemed to shake the whole house on its foundations as she threw herself across her bed. Slade had gone, but she was too full of misery to care. He had achieved what he had come for, so he couldn't complain. If he was angry that she hadn't completely succumbed to his charms, no doubt he would get over it. Nothing daunted him for long; she had ordered him out, but he would be laughing over it by now. He would regard her as a nuisance successfully got rid of, and would probably be trying to decide which of his beautiful girl-friends to take out to dinner.

Lee groaned, trying not to notice the horrible black jealousy that swept over her as she thought of him dining with another woman. It had been easier to send him away than it was to banish him from her thoughts. Feverishly she clasped her hands together and found she couldn't even rely on the comfort of her engagement ring any more. Slade had removed it through the night, flinging it over the room as if he couldn't bear to see it on her finger any longer. She had been going to look for it this morning, to put it somewhere safe until she could give it back to Matt, but somehow she had forgotten all about it. Now the bareness of her left hand both taunted and reproached her as she recalled Slade's derisive words. If she had loved Matt how could she have let Slade make love to her? Unfortunately she loved the wrong man!

She wasn't aware that Slade was standing looking at her until he spoke. She was so utterly distraught and sobbing so loudly that it was several seconds before his voice penetrated through the abandoned noise she was making. When it did, she gasped and buried her head in a pillow, rather than let him see her tear-drenched face.

'I didn't want to give you another fright,' he said tautly, and she felt the bed give to his weight as he sat down beside her.

Why had he come back? He sounded as if something had driven him back against his will. Whatever it was must have had a pretty powerful effect, for there had been anger in the force with which he had slammed the front door.

'I told you . . .' she choked.

'Hush!' She suddenly felt herself lifted into his arms with her hot face pressed to the smoothness of his shirt while one of his hands caressed the back of her head and neck. 'Hush,' he said again, his voice oddly uneven. 'Did you really believe I could go away, leaving you like this?'

With an effort she controlled her sobs, but rejected an inclination to cling to him. 'What difference can it make?' she whispered.

'I'm not sure,' he sighed, resting his cheek on the top of her head as he folded her closer. 'I only know I couldn't bear seeing you so upset. I can't promise we might reach a better understanding.'

'How could we reach a better understanding,' she countered bitterly, 'when you're so determined to destroy what little happiness I have left?'

'That's the last thing I'd want to do.'

'You came here for that sole purpose.'

'No, Lee.' As if frustratingly seeking a more explicit way to deny it, he released her gently and stood up to pace to the window before returning to her side. This time, as Lee huddled against her pillows, she didn't try and hide her swollen face, but surprisingly he didn't appear to find anything wrong with it. With her hair all tumbled, her robe rumpled, she must have looked in a total state of dishevelment, yet he was staring at her with all the admiration in his eyes that had been evident when she had been dressed in her best to go out with him in New York. And there was something else that might easily have been mistaken for tenderness. She wondered if he was aware of it.

At last he broke the strained silence. 'I'm not completely sure why I came here last night, Lee. There are some things I don't know the answer to myself, but

I'm not so hardened that I enjoy making anyone miserable.'

She stared at him, swallowing another sob. This was probably as near to an apology as he would ever get. She tried to accept it but couldn't. 'Wouldn't it be nearer the truth to say you came back to gloat? There can't be many as easily duped as I've been.'

'Lee!' he said, with a harshness that betrayed a certain reluctance. 'I'll admit, when I returned here, it was for the sole purpose of destroying your engagement to Matt. It was quite a shock to discover I still wanted you for myself. Even then, I wasn't going further than a few kisses.'

'Then why did you?' she gulped.

'Why did I?' he frowned, as if he was asking himself the same question. 'I suppose, after I kissed you, I saw no reason to deny myself and things got out of control.' His eyes smouldered as they lingered on the softness of her lips, then moved slowly to the fulness of her breasts, clearly outlined under the thinness of her robe. 'You don't realise how beautiful you are, Lee. You've been in my blood ever since I first saw you. I've wanted you ever since.'

'You used blackmail to get me, five years ago.'

He stared into her accusing eyes. 'I wanted you insanely, my love, and I've always been an opportunist. You were a thief, and there was plenty of evidence to suggest you'd been involved with other men. I thought what I was offering was, on the whole, extremely generous.'

'I wasn't a thief,' uneasily she bit a lip, 'only I couldn't tell you.'

He watched her carefully. Lee wasn't aware that her eyes were almost convincing him she was telling the truth but that his knowledge of women had taught him to be wary. 'You could have challenged me to do my worst,' he said dryly.

'You could have sent me to prison!'

He smiled. 'You must have realised I wouldn't do that. That was why I was almost certain you came to me willingly.'

It was too near what she suspected herself to think about. Instead she hid her confusion with more accusations. 'When I lived with you, you watched me all the time. You never trusted me, not even with other men.'

He drew a deep breath and his jaw tensed. 'I knew there hadn't been anyone before me, although it was a shock to discover you were a virgin, but after we were together, Lee, you developed quite an appetite for making love. I'd never known a more passionate woman. I couldn't believe you'd be satisfied with only me.'

'There's just been one man in my whole life,' she cried, mortified that he should think such vile things of her. Her face flushed, she choked. 'Not even Matt . . .'

'I know!' he threw up an almost pleading hand. 'After the first shock had worn off, your innocence pleased me greatly. It still does, all these years later, to find you've belonged only to me. As for not trusting you, otherwise—well, what would you expect?' he shrugged. 'Having caught you trying to steal my mother's jewellery, or at least knowing you'd been tempted to, I tried to make sure, for both our sakes, that it didn't happen again.'

# CHAPTER FIVE

LEE stared at him, eyes filled with remembered anguish. 'You don't know what your constant suspicion did to me. That and the position I was in.'

Slade sat on the bed beside her again and stroked her hand. 'We were two people living together, Lee, there's nothing so terrible about that. If you'd been older you wouldn't have felt as you did. You certainly wouldn't have run away.'

'Did you ever look for me?' she asked suddenly.

'Look for you?' he repeated carefully, avoiding her unconsciously eager glance. 'I believe I made one or two enquiries, but it seemed better to let you go, as that was obviously what you wanted.'

Was the sudden pallor of his face relevant? Lee thought not. It more likely had to do with the fact that he'd been travelling almost non-stop for the last few days and it was just catching up on him.

'Well,' she said heavily, 'that's all behind me now, though it hasn't been easy.'

He nodded understandingly. 'I can imagine these past few years haven't been easy, but I intend making it up to you. You would never have been happy with Matt, but that doesn't mean you have to be deprived of a man again.'

Flushing with indignation, she frowned at him. 'I don't think I like the sound of that!'

'Maybe I put it rather indelicately,' he smiled expansively. 'I'm talking about you and me.'

Her frown turned to a glare. Slade was impossible, conceited and arrogant. How had she ever come to love him? He might be proposing, but it was doubtful—he valued his freedom too much. 'What do you mean— you and me?'

'Just that.' Confidently, he lifted her hand to his lips. Over her taut knuckles he stared straight into her eyes. 'I want you, Lee, more than ever, and I'm going to be here for several weeks. I intend seeing you whenever I can spare the time.'

She had underestimated his conceit! 'Could you manage every night?' she asked silkily, retrieving her hand.

'I don't see why not. And sometimes through the day,' he grinned, the prospect clearly pleasing him.

Lee ground her teeth in fury. 'You can go to hell!' she said, very slowly and distinctly.

'That's not very ladylike,' he reproved mildly, to Lee's chagrin not taking her seriously.

'When did you ever think I was a lady!' she shouted. 'Lee . . .!'

'If you had, you wouldn't be making such a proposition.'

'You're an odd mixture, aren't you?' he quirked wryly. 'So strait-laced in some ways and anything but in others.'

'I'm probably just normal,' she retorted, her anger increasing as she felt her cheeks growing hot. 'But I don't want to live with you again. I don't want that kind of relationship any more. I don't think I ever did. It was forced on me!'

Slade sighed at her outburst but still refused to take her seriously. 'I'll give you anything you want. You can't deny I've always been extremely generous. You never lost anything.'

'Only my self-respect!'

'You're exaggerating,' he said, with a little less patience.

'No, I'm not!' she denied fiercely. 'And if I was fool enough to see you while you're here, what happens when you go away? You'll forget all about me again.'

'It won't be like that,' he argued, eyes darkening.

'You will come with me. We can travel all over the world, as we did before.'

Wildly she shook her head. 'It would never work,' she cried. 'You don't even love me!'

He frowned. 'I have a certain feeling for you, Lee.'

'But—not love?'

His face closed, as she had known it would, but he moved determinedly nearer, clasping her shoulders this time, instead of her hands. 'What we have, my darling, will hold us together better than this other foolish emotion you talk of. It's far stronger, for one thing.'

'How do you know?'

'I can prove it to you,' he insisted, his eyes beginning to smoulder.

'No!' She wriggled to escape, wishing her heart wouldn't beat so crazily whenever he touched her. 'I don't want to listen to you. I wish you'd leave. This conversation is getting us nowhere.'

He laughed lightly and bent his head, brushing his mouth over angry lips. 'You have no choice but to listen to me, my sexy little wildcat. I refuse to let you go.'

'Stop it, Slade!' she cried, twisting away frantically before he had her senses whirling. 'I don't want you!'

'Of course you do,' he murmured, pulling her back to him remorselessly, his lips grazing the side of her cheek as she furiously turned her head and settling against her earlobe. Strange darts of fire began running down her neck, connecting with places she didn't want to think of, but when she began beating at him with her fists, his only reaction was to begin kissing her in earnest.

As familiar sensations started flooding through her, Lee might have given in at once if she hadn't been so incensed at the way he used brute force to override her objections. She tried to insert her hand between them to push him away, but he controlled her wild struggles with an ease that had her clawing hysterically at his face and shoulders.

With a half strangled oath, his amusement faded and
he flung himself on top of her, pressing down on her
until she lay in a breathless state of acquiescence
beneath him.

'I hate you!' she moaned.

He laughed mockingly. 'Let me show you how
much!'

She could have hit him as his mouth passionately
assaulted hers and he proved beyond doubt what she
didn't want to believe. She didn't hate him, she wanted
him every bit as much as he wanted her, and she
shivered with despair as she felt the violent stirrings of
desire again. When he lifted his head to let them both
breathe, she was wildly flushed and trembling, with her
arms around his neck in a feverish grip.

'What did I tell you?' he murmured, eyes alight with
satisfaction.

Numbly she gazed at him as he began slowly slipping
the robe from her shoulders, his intentions very obvious
as the extent of his arousal became clear to her. 'Slade,'
she gasped, 'we can't! Your work—you must have
people to see . . .'

'It's Saturday, my love,' he said thickly, devouring
her with his eyes as her robe hit the floor. 'I have no
definite appointments, apart from Matt, this afternoon.
If I had, they could go to hell as far as I'm concerned.
You're far more important.'

'But . . .'

'Be quiet,' he retorted, his voice ragged as he threw
off his own clothes. 'I don't want to talk about it.
We've better things to do.'

This wasn't sensible! Lee shuddered. Why couldn't
she say no to him and mean it? Tears of frustration ran
down her cheeks and she quivered as he kissed them
away. His mouth was tender and moist, consuming her
with rapture until her head became cloudy and only
filled with the impatience of waiting. She trembled as
his hand stroked her hip and thigh, increasing her sense

of longing. With shaking fingers she began helping him to remove his shirt, returning his kisses passionately between the releasing of each button. Their eyes met and held, savouring the exquisite torture of ecstasy delayed, their bodies at a fever-pitch of wanting.

He leaned across her, his hard chest solid against her yielding softness, and as he rolled her into his arms she gloried at her ability to excite this man and that he could still give her so much pleasure. He held her tightly until her body blazed from the heat of his and she flung her arms around his neck again, wildly whispering his name.

His mouth found hers with almost savage force as he finally claimed her and they began moving together in a primitive rhythm that was soul-shaking in its very intensity. Lee felt she must surely be consumed by the tension within her, until such feelings were shattered and dwarfed by the ultimate ones of devastating ecstasy.

Later they drank tea together in the kitchen and ate toast. It wasn't surprising that they were hungry as they had both discovered they had had nothing to eat since the day before. Slade confessed that he had had dinner, but Lee hadn't. There wasn't time for anything more substantial as Slade, despite his recent denial, had remembered a midday appointment and Lee recalled having promised to visit the Mansfields for coffee.

'I'm going to be late!' she exclaimed, hurrying to the garage with Slade strolling beside her.

'Does it matter?' he muttered, reluctant to let her out of his sight. 'Why don't we just drop everything and go to Paris for the weekend?'

'Non, monsieur,' she replied in her quick French which, for some reason, had always amused him. She was determined not to be enticed. Did he still remember the enchantment of Paris? He had once said he had never realised its magic until he had been there with her.

He didn't seem too disturbed by her refusal. 'We can

go another time,' he smiled, clearly believing she was now his to command exactly as he liked.

Firmly she shook her head, ignoring his look of frowning disbelief as she briefly reiterated what she had said earlier. 'Please don't argue, Slade,' she begged. 'There isn't time, and I won't change my mind.'

'I don't care about the time, or how long it takes!' he retorted curtly, his arms shooting out to swing her around to him as they entered the old tile-roofed garage. 'What sort of a woman are you?' he jeered. 'Five minutes ago you were begging me not to leave you. Now you don't want to see me again.'

She flushed and stared at the worn stone floor, wishing he would at least try and understand. Of course, the thing was, he didn't want to understand! He knew she couldn't resist him when he got this close, but he would rather believe she was wanton . . .

Anger returning, she flung back her head. 'I won't be your mistress, Slade.'

'Don't you think you should think it over?' he smiled, his glance softer, as though her tempestuous beauty wouldn't allow him to be annoyed with her for long.

She stared at him, mutely shaking her head. If only he wasn't so good-looking, she thought. Why did this one man contain so much magnetism for her that though she had so recently been in his arms, she yearned to be in them again?

'We could have a wonderful time, my darling.' The confidence in Slade's voice increased as he saw her falter. 'How about a few weeks in the Caribbean?'

'Shut up! Be quiet!' she cried wildly, putting her hands over her ears to drown anything more out, while her blue eyes turned purple and sparked at him feverishly. 'I won't be bought, I tell you! You can keep your money!'

'Diamonds—furs?' he tempted, wrenching her hands away, forcing her to listen. 'Once you couldn't get enough of them, so what's bugging you?'

'You are!' she choked. 'You come here with your arrogant ways and think you can order me around and treat me like dirt. If you believe I'm not good enough for your cousin, why should you contaminate yourself by having another affair with me?'

His face hardened. 'I hope this childish display of temper doesn't mean you intend carrying on with your engagement?'

Lee wished she could say it did. 'No,' she said tightly, 'I promised I'd tell Matt and I will, as soon as I can.'

His narrowed eyes studied her beautiful but wilful face for several moments before seeming satisfied. 'You can get rid of that deplorable machine, too,' he nodded towards her motorcycle, 'as soon as you like. Otherwise I'll do it for you.'

Lee blinked incredulously. The power he thought he had over her was going to his head! 'You can't dictate my whole life!' she snapped, reaching deliberately for her helmet.

His temper rose as swiftly as her own. 'Your grandfather ought to have had his brains examined for buying it for you!'

Lee jumped quickly to her grandfather's defence. 'He didn't buy it specially for me,' she explained resentfully. 'It belonged to one of his Italian waiters who got a phone call one day to say his father was seriously ill and he asked Grandfather to loan him some money so he could fly home. He promised to pay it back, but we never saw him again. He did write, though, telling Grandfather he could keep the bike.'

'Which he should have sold or given to charity, rather than let you have it.'

'I was very young, Slade,' she said shortly, 'And I only rode it over the fields. It was fun, and Giulio had taught me.'

'Even at that age,' Slade scorned, 'you were twisting men around your little finger.'

'But not you,' she couldn't help remarking.

His eyes darkened. 'I'd like to believe it.'

Lee was anxious to leave him, she had no wish to prolong such a conversation. She hadn't used the Honda again until her grandfather died, when the terrible anguish of losing not only Slade but her grandfather as well had really begun hitting her. She had found that the concentration required to ride it safely had helped to give her temporary respite from her grief. Then, when she had started to look for material to illustrate her books, she had used it to reach places not readily accessible by road. Sandra had liked to come with her occasionally, when she had the day off and Julia was working, but she seemed to have lost her enthusiasm for such outings since Lee had got engaged to Matt. Lee didn't know why she was taking it to The Willows, this morning, when she had intended using her car. Slade's scathing remarks might have something to do with it, but she had no intention of changing her mind. It was important that he realised that any influence he had over her began and stopped with Matt.

As she began fastening her helmet, eyes sparkling cool defiance, Slade ripped it off again. With an infuriating smile, he confiscated her spare one as well, and carrying them both, started walking towards his car, believing he was putting an effective end to any more opposition.

Lee saw red. Jumping on to the Honda, she jerked it off its stand and kicked the starter. The engine immediately responded, allowing her to roar straight past Slade, missing him by inches. He was forced to jump out of her way and because of the two helmets he was carrying, lost his balance and fell heavily against the metal fittings of the up-and-over door.

A feeling of fear hit Lee, but she didn't stop. He was too strong to be seriously injured by a little fall like that, and if she went back to see they would only be at each other's throats again.

It was breaking the law as well as dangerous to ride

without a helmet. When she realised what she was doing, Lee almost turned back, but the roads were deserted and if she didn't waste any time she might get to The Willows without anyone seeing her.

She was lucky, she didn't pass a single car, and fortunately no one at The Willows witnessed her arrival. How she was going to leave, minus a helmet, she had yet to work out.

'We'd given you up!' Dulcie complained. 'It's a good job George won't be in for lunch.'

George owned a recording company where all his energy seemed to be spent. 'They're recording the Ice Spots,' Trigg said proudly. 'You like them, don't you, Lee?'

'They're very popular,' hedged Lee, wondering what Slade was doing and hoping that the knock he had got on his head might have knocked some sense into it!

'Can I go and see your bike, Lee, if I promise not to get on it?' asked Trigg, after they had all talked about the leading groups for a while and he had obviously lost interest.

'Yes,' Lee gave her permission, having the keys in her pocket. 'As long as you're careful and your mother doesn't mind?' She took care to consult Dulcie this time.

Dulcie shook her head, looking glad to be rid of him. She led the way to the kitchen, where she passed Lee a weak mug of coffee that tasted as if it might have been made hours ago.

'Do you mind?' After a second unsuccessful attempt to drink it, Lee poured what was left of it down the sink, then switched on the kettle after checking that it was full of water. Reaching for the Nescafé, she said, 'I feel like something hot and strong. I'll bring you another jar.'

'You'd better,' Dulcie grumbled. 'I'm not made of money. And you can make me another cup, too, while you're at it. I've had a terrible morning.'

Could it have been worse than hers? Lee glanced at Dulcie ironically. But for Trigg, it was doubtful if they would have been more than passing acquaintances. They had so little in common they would never be close friends, but sometimes Dulcie had a lost look about her that seemed a curious reflection of something in herself.

'We all have terrible mornings occasionally,' she said lightly, having no real wish to hear details of a domestic crisis which probably existed only in Dulcie's imagination.

'Will Trigg be all right?' Dulcie asked suddenly, clearly resenting Lee's lack of immediate sympathy. 'I know I said he could look at your bike, but he's taking his time. I hope he's not up to something. Really, Lee,' she fretted, 'after what happened the other night, I do wish you'd had the sense to leave it at home!'

'He can't come to any harm,' smiled Lee. 'I have the keys in my pocket.' She fished them out. 'See?'

'Couldn't he hurt himself, though?'

'I hardly think so,' Lee soothed, 'but I'll go and take a look.'

'No!' Dulcie stopped her hastily. 'I daresay you're right, and we can have a more enjoyable chat while we're on our own.'

Lee forbore to say it was Trigg she had come to see. The kettle boiled and she made two more mugs of coffee. It was hot this time, and while Dulcie sipped elegantly, she gulped hers down, feeling she hadn't been exaggerating when she'd said she needed it. After that last scene with Slade, she probably needed something stronger, but the coffee did help.

Almost as if she had known Lee was thinking of him, Dulcie asked softly, 'Have you seen that gorgeous Mr Western again?'

'Yes.' Lee would have given anything to have been able to say no.

'I've discovered he's in electronics and he's got microchip plants all over the place.' Dulcie's smile was a mixture of awe and admiration. 'It's the up-and-coming thing, you know. I hear he's big in America.'

'So I believe,' Lee agreed noncommittally.

'George says he must be worth something.'

'Probably.' Lee pretended to be bored. 'How's Trigg getting on at school?'

Dulcie sighed impatiently but answered readily enough. 'Not bad. As soon as his health improves we're sending him to George's old one. I must admit it would be a relief. He had a bad attack yesterday and had to stay at home. I managed to get out to have my hair done, but I was worried all the time. It quite spoiled my day.'

'You didn't leave Trigg here alone!'

'God,' breathed Dulcie angrily, 'you people without kids are all the same—always criticising! Wait until you have some of your own, then you'll realise it's far from easy.'

Lee was saved from having to apologise, for Trigg's sake, by his unexpected arrival. He burst into the kitchen, his freckled face unusually excited.

'That man's here again, Lee!' he panted. 'The one who put us in the ditch. There's a truck, too. They're taking your bike!'

'Trigg!' Dulcie intervened in a startled voice, but Lee was already halfway through the door with an unheeding Trigg closely on her heels.

What was Slade doing? Or was Trigg having her on? She hadn't heard anything, but that wasn't surprising as Dulcie always had the radio going full blast with the volume turned up.

As she raced outside, around the corner of the house, she saw Slade's car first, then the truck. Trigg hadn't been joking after all. Her bike was on it and a man in a boiler suit was banging the tail-board in place. He was using the heel of his hand and some choice language when he hurt his thumb. Slade stood watching, an expression of grim satisfaction on his face.

'What on earth do you think you're doing?' cried Lee, hair flying, eyes blazing as she skidded to a halt. 'Who are you?' she rounded on the man in the boiler suit.

He looked embarrassed, but Slade didn't. 'Get going, Johnston, and follow my instructions precisely,' he said. 'Leave the—er—lady to me.'

Had Slade hesitated deliberately? Lee could never remember feeling so outraged. 'No, wait a minute!' she grabbed the man's arm. 'That's my property you're busy loading up. It has nothing to do with anyone else,' she shot Slade an icy glance. 'You're taking it away without my authority, which amounts to stealing, and if you don't unload it at once, I'll call the police!'

'I shouldn't advise it,' Slade cautioned smoothly, moving closer so she could see the dark bruise on the side of his face. 'Unless you want me to take advantage of their proximity. I might also be tempted to tell them a few things!'

Lee glared at him, seeing him totting them up. Knocking him down, riding without lights and now a helmet. The light bulb hadn't been replaced and her helmets were, no doubt, still in the boot of his car. 'I may have committed one or two minor offences, but nothing to justify the confiscation of my bike!'

'I'm doing it for your own sake, as well as that of others.' He glanced pointedly at Trigg, who was being firmly restrained by his mother, several yards away.

'You aren't being reasonable,' she choked.

'As reasonable as you deserve,' he snapped, raising an insinuating hand to his bruised face.

Uncomfortably she turned to him, just long enough to allow his unhelpful accomplice to escape. With a curious but brief nod the man climbed into the truck and hurtled off, leaving Lee waving after him furiously.

'I'll sue you for this!' She flew at Slade, cheeks scarlet. 'You had no business . . .'

'You are my business.' Taking no notice of Dulcie, as if he didn't care who heard, he grasped Lee's flailing hands. 'You aren't fit to look after yourself, Lee, and if you're through making an exhibition of yourself, I'll take you home.'

'What are you going to do with Lee's bike, Mr Western?' Trigg asked unhappily, edging forward. 'If you don't like her having it, I could look after it for her.'

'No, you couldn't!' Dulcie's hands tightened on her son's shoulders. 'Neither you nor Lee has any sense. Someone should have done what Mr Western's done long ago.'

Slade smiled at her. 'I'm glad you agree.'

'Of course I do!' Dulcie basked in the warmth of his approval.

'Will you sell it?' asked Trigg.

'Scrap it, more likely,' Slade answered grimly. 'Either way, Lee will get what it brings.'

Lee had enough sense to recognise that there was nothing to be gained by standing here arguing. They were merely arousing Dulcie's curiosity, and she already had plenty to keep her talking for weeks! Slade didn't seem to mind, but she refused to provide any more free entertainment. 'I'm going home,' she announced abruptly, 'but by myself.' She glanced at Slade coldly. 'You can't expect me to accept your offer of a lift after what you've just done.'

'I said I'll take you!' His hand shot to her arm before she could avoid it.

'Won't you both stay for lunch?' Dulcie asked hastily, but Slade didn't appear to hear her. He thrust Lee so unceremoniously into his car that before she could find the breath to get out again he was in beside her and roaring off.

When she did recover her breath she attacked him wildly. 'Of all the rude, outrageous men I've ever had the misfortune to meet, you're the worst! Not content with ruining my life, you've now resorted to stealing my property . . .'

'Call me a thief,' he interrupted curtly, 'and I'll have to remind you of something.'

As if she could ever forget! And he was quite capable of backing up any story he told the police with information regarding her earlier crimes! Colour slid from her face. 'Blackmailing again?'

'You provoke me to it.' His glittering glance was full of anger. 'We both know there's no possibility of blackmail, but until you learn to conduct yourself in a civilised manner, you mustn't object if I react in a similar fashion.'

A civilised manner? Her eyes flew suddenly to the side of his face where the dark bruise was spreading. Her anger faded as she felt his pain herself. 'Did I do that, Slade?'

'Yes,' his lips formed a cynical curve. 'I blame myself, though—I must be getting senile if I can't remember your ungovernable temper. Another woman might have responded reasonably to the advice I was giving for your own sake. But not you! I caught a glimpse of the murderous glint in your eyes—you would have liked to have killed me.'

Her voice shook. 'No, never! You certainly made me angry, but I didn't mean to harm you. I might have given that impression, but it was more a case of not realising what I was doing.'

'I'd like to believe it.'

'You can.' She felt stricken that he expressed such a lack of trust. Was there no area where she could count on it? 'Slade,' she faltered, 'I know my bike has been a sore point between us, but surely you don't mean to keep it?'

'I do.'

He sounded so uncompromising that she flinched. 'But why?'

'Why?' he drawled, turning into her drive. 'Because I still happen to want you, and I'm not prepared to let you go on risking your neck.'

Want, want, want! Lee's stomach muscles tightened.
That was all she ever heard from Slade. Hadn't he
already taken enough? 'Don't you think you've got
your strategy wrong?' she taunted. 'You're only
succeeding in driving me away.'

'That wasn't the impression I received through the
night,' he mocked.

'You'd be wiser,' she retorted bitterly, 'not to put
your trust in that.'

He drew up so sharply before River Bend that Lee
was flung abruptly forward. 'What was that for?' she
cried.

'Perhaps just to remind you,' he said smoothly, as she
brushed back the hair that had fallen over her face,
'that I don't care for opposition of any kind. I've got
rid of that infernal machine that endangered your life.
Now all you've got to do is get rid of Matt.'

'Slade!' she began to protest.

'Shush! Not another word.' As she opened her mouth
to speak, his hand moved to jerk her against his
unyielding body.

It was a casual display of power that had her fighting
for breath. He was imposing his will on her. Ever since
he had come back he had been doing it all the time,
showing her how far she could go. Tears forced their
way into her eyes; she turned pale but tightened her lips
against a murmur of pain. He stared at her for a long
moment until his pupils began to darken. His mouth
tightened as he dealt impatiently with the emotion
causing it and abruptly loosened his hold.

Lee drew a deep breath, cautiously moving her head
to try and release the tension in her neck. As though her
helplessness excited him, Slade slid a hand under her
hair, probing beneath the collar of her shirt to find the
silk of her skin. Her breath caught as he traced the top
of her spine with delicate care, sending showers of
sensation over her.

Feeling her shiver, he laughed softly, yet it was with a

harsher sound that he lifted her chin and forced her mouth to endure the suddenly heated invasion of his. His lips pushed at hers, edging them apart, and whatever protest she had been about to utter was lost in the flood of sentient response that rose from the pit of her stomach. Involuntarily she arched against him and felt the tremor that went through his body, the immediate tightening of his muscles which denoted his heightening desire.

'You're mine!' he muttered, holding her tightly, his voice thick. 'I want you, and whatever it is between us, it's not going to go away. You know that as well as I do.'

'No, Slade!' she pleaded, reminded sharply of what she was doing. 'You're insane!'

Air rushed out of him as her continuing refusal to listen infuriated him. 'There seems to be only one way I can make you believe,' he snapped, lowering his head.

His lips scorched her cheeks as he found her mouth while curses rasped between his teeth. While her own breath was trapped beneath the fierce possession of his kiss, he bent her back until she was pinned against the seat both by his weight and mounting passion. He demanded a response she would have been reluctant to give, but as always her body betrayed her. Slade's ruthlessness shocked her, but she was even more shocked by the signs inside her that warned that her resistance was useless. Her blood was surging and boiling too feverishly to be of any help in fighting him. Her inarticulate cries faded and she moaned as he ripped open the front of her shirt and his hands closed over her palpitating breasts.

The pressure inside her increased as his fingers stroked and he continued to arouse her. She clung to him as he kissed her lips with unhurried pleasure, then buried his face against her racing heartbeats. She had only to turn slightly to help his searching mouth find her nipple. In an agony of suspense she waited before his lips closed over it.

Making a deep sound in her throat, she moved hungrily against him, but felt stunned when his muscles tensed and after a few taut seconds, during which his grip threatened to break her, he put her firmly aside. He didn't do it easily. His jaw clenched and with glazed eyes she saw him fighting the overwhelming temptation of her very feminine sensuality as well as his own.

'Wh-what's wrong?' she stammered, flushing deeply as she realised how much her query revealed.

Slade smiled as he straightened. 'Nothing now,' he said softly. 'The only obstacle remaining is Matt, and you'll tell him, won't you?'

'Yes,' she promised, envying Slade's swift return to normality but with no fight left in her to make a cutting remark about it.

'You won't regret it,' he brushed a quick kiss over her uncertain lips. 'I'll be in touch.'

Lee watched him drive away with some misgivings which she tried to ignore. For the rest of the day she did her best to nurture the faint hope that once she was free again Slade might ask her to marry him. Perhaps he didn't love her, but he must care for her a little, otherwise why had he bothered himself so much over her bike?

Lee thought about her bike, but, apart from a lingering feeling of outrage over the way in which Slade had set about it, she wasn't really sorry that it had gone. She had outgrown it. For a long time she had thought of getting rid of it, it was only young Trigg's interest in it that had made her keep putting off. He reminded Lee of herself at his age. Her mother had been possessive over her but had never really wanted her. Trigg's parents were the same. They were prepared to give him anything other than their time and attention. Sometimes she wondered how much they loved him. She must have a word with Dulcie about boarding school. Dulcie must know he was fretting over it. He was quite happy in his present school where his

teachers understood his asthmatic condition and helped
him to cope with it. Other staff at another school
would, but Trigg wasn't sure of this and it made him
unhappy.

She waited for Matt that evening with some
trepidation. After showering, she put on a short skirt
and blouse which she topped with a loose sweater, as
the air since teatime had turned distinctly chilly. Matt
and she often went out on Saturday nights and they
usually dressed up, but Matt wouldn't wonder long
over her rather austere appearance when he heard what
she had to tell him.

He arrived at seven, earlier than usual, but when she
heard his car she went to meet him. She saw
immediately that something was wrong and a terrible
coldness suddenly invaded her. Had Slade told him the
truth, this afternoon, after they had finished discussing
business? He had said he wouldn't. He hadn't actually
promised, but she had believed him. She would rather
have told Matt herself, but he looked so grim that this
seemed the only possible explanation.

'Matt?' she whispered fearfully, wondering exactly
what Slade had said, her blue eyes widening apprehensively as she clung to the doorknob with both
hands, 'You—you seem disturbed about something.
Won't you come in?'

'It's my father,' he replied, without moving, apart
from rubbing a weary hand over his brow. 'He's ill
again. Mother rang just as I was leaving and I promised
I'd go as soon as I'd called here and seen you.'

# CHAPTER SIX

'OH.' Lee looked at him blankly, his father's illness scarcely registering. So Slade hadn't said anything, after all. She felt briefly ashamed for doubting him but still in a quandary. Matt was in a hurry and anxious. How could she tell him she couldn't marry him, right now? It just wouldn't be fair!

'Yes, of course you must go,' she laid a sympathetic hand on his arm. 'Would you like me to come with you?'

'No, I don't think so,' he squeezed her hand absently as he hesitated uncomfortably. 'I believe Mother would rather I went by myself. She gets great relief from just being able to talk to me, you see. She doesn't find it easy to discuss her personal problems with someone else around.'

Lee nodded, keeping her private thoughts to herself. Perhaps it was just as well she wasn't going to be Mrs Leland's daughter-in-law, but she would have been marrying Matt, not his mother. It said a lot for Matt that he was so willing to consider his parents, without being dominated by them. He was simply a warm, caring person, which didn't make Lee feel any prouder of what she had done.

'It's a pity Sandra isn't here,' she said ruefully. 'She might have been able to give some practical advice.'

'Mother would have welcomed her,' Matt agreed. 'Because of her being a nurse, you know,' he added quickly.

'Will I see you later?' Lee walked to the car with him when he refused to come in for a drink.

'We'd better leave it until tomorrow.' He kissed her swiftly. 'I've been saying that too often lately, haven't I?'

95

He rang at ten to say his father was keeping better but that his mother wanted him to stay the night. He would see Lee the next day.

She lay awake for hours that night and just seemed to have got to sleep when she was wakened by the phone. Thinking it must be Matt, with an emergency on his hands, she groped too quickly for the receiver and dropped it as she was picking it up.

'What was that all about?' a voice asked, but it wasn't Matt's.

'Slade!'

'Hello, Lee,' he said softly. 'Still in bed?'

'I had a bad night.' He sounded as if he would liked to have been in bed beside her, and she put a hand over her heart to try and calm the sudden wildness of its beat.

'Because of me?'

'You flatter yourself,' she retorted sharply. 'Why did you ring, Slade?'

'I should have thought you could have guessed,' he taunted. 'I want to know if you've told Matt.'

Sensing menacing undertones, she shivered. 'Not yet.'

'Why not?' he snapped.

'It wasn't my fault,' she bridled. 'You don't think I could possibly go on being engaged to Matt after what—what's . . .'

'Happened,' Slade supplied bluntly. 'You don't have to get in such a state, Lee. There's nothing to be ashamed of. You belong to me, you always have and always will, but as usual you're evading the issue. I want to know why you haven't told him yet.'

'His father's ill.' Lee pushed at her hair with agitated fingers. 'He called, but he had to go and help. You surely wouldn't expect me to tell a man I couldn't marry him in those circumstances? He was worried and in a hurry.'

'You could have asked him to call later.'

'I did!' She took a deep breath to control her rising temper. 'He said we'd better leave it.'

'Has he always put his family before you?'

Slade's cynicism drove her to retort, 'Other men do.'

He was immediately, blazingly angry. 'I'm afraid I find it difficult to believe you want to tell Matt anything. I warned you, Lee, I won't allow you to keep putting off. When I see him tomorrow if he doesn't know by then that you aren't going to marry him, then I'll tell him myself.'

Had she taken leave of her senses? Lee wondered all morning. The deed was done, she had betrayed Matt with another man and must learn to live with the consequences of her own folly. Yet, though she knew she couldn't marry Matt now, loving Slade as she did, an empty future was not one she found easy to face.

Matt came after lunch. His father had recovered and his mother was feeling better. He looked tired, but so pleased to be with her that Lee felt worse than ever.

'I'm so glad about your dad!' She gave him a quick hug, for, whatever happened, she would always be fond of him. But when he sought to prolong the embrace, she mumbled an apology for not ringing and dragged him into the lounge.

'Why didn't you?' Matt glanced at her rather reproachfully as he slumped into a chair. 'I thought you might.'

'I didn't want to disturb anyone.' Lee patted a cushion on another chair, rearranging it unnecessarily as she wondered if there was any best way of breaking an engagement.

'Isn't Sandra back yet?' enquired Matt, doing little to conceal a gigantic yawn.

'I'm expecting her this evening.'

'Mother wondered if she'd have time to look in.' He frowned with a hint of bewilderment. 'I don't know why it should always be Sandra, but she seems anxious to see her.'

'I'll tell her as soon as she comes in,' Lee promised absently.

Matt didn't seem to notice she talked as though he wouldn't be here. 'We could all go over for half an hour,' he suggested eagerly, then patted the arm of his chair, looking more relaxed. 'Come and tell me what you've been doing with yourself this weekend. Pounding your typewriter, I suppose?'

Lee smiled faintly in response to his rather heavy humour but pretended she hadn't noticed the invitation his hand was patting out. He wouldn't want her that close when he heard what she had to say.

'Matt,' she began unhappily, 'I'm afraid I've something to tell you that might come as a shock.'

To her astonishment, because she was shaking, he didn't appear to take her seriously. He yawned again, looking ready to fall asleep. 'Unless it's something that absolutely won't keep, darling, I'd rather you told me another time. I've had a bad spell at home, and before that a hectic session with Slade. I don't know what's got into him! I could swear he had something on his mind that had nothing to do with business. I didn't like the way he stalked about his office, when I was there, and I'm not fond of having to repeat everything twice. Then, last night, I realise I hadn't visited my parents for a few days, but you'd think it had been years! Mother never stopped complaining. You'd think she was the only one with problems.'

'Matt,' Lee looked at him shamefacedly, trying to keep her mind on him and not Slade. 'What I have to say can't wait. This might come as a terrible surprise—but I want to end our engagement.'

He frowned, staring at her uncomprehendingly. 'Is this some kind of joke?'

'No.' Watching confusion filling his dazed eyes, she hated what she was doing to him. 'I only wish it had been.'

He went very pale and jerked upright from his lounging position. She saw him swallow, then he said, 'I do believe you mean it, Lee.'

'I do,' she confirmed, her voice little more than a whisper.

'You're sure?'

'Yes.'

Matt sat where he was a moment longer. There was a brief silence, then he rose to his feet. 'Am I allowed to ask why?'

Lee was relieved that he sounded slightly acid; she had been afraid he might break down. Nevertheless, she still hated herself for what she was doing to him and couldn't bring herself to insult him with less than the truth. 'I've discovered I don't love you.'

He frowned. 'I thought you did, and you aren't the kind of girl whose feelings change overnight . . .'

Her eyes filled with tears. 'I'm not, Matt. I thought I loved you, then I suddenly realised it wasn't the right kind of love for marriage. It seemed only fair to tell you.'

'Of course.' He seemed to understand that her tears were for him yet he looked completely baffled. 'Is there—someone else?'

'No.' How could she say there was when the man involved had no serious intentions?

Matt accepted this. He slipped the ring she gave back to him into his pocket; Lee was relieved that he didn't ask her to keep it as a memento. He said hoarsely, 'I may look no different, but I feel as though I'd been hit by a bus.'

'I'm sorry, Matt,' she whispered, gazing at him helplessly. 'I—I hope you'll soon meet someone who really deserves you.'

His mouth twisted. 'I'll never meet anyone as wonderful as you, Lee.' Pausing, he exclaimed, 'I haven't done or said something I'm not aware of, Lee? I don't always realise . . .'

She shook her head quickly. 'If there had been, Matt, I would have asked you about it. I would have given you a chance to explain. I'm usually the one who speaks without thinking.'

'My mother?' he hesitated. 'I know she isn't easy.'

'She had nothing to do with my decision,' Lee assured him firmly. 'She and I would have got on. We aren't such bad friends as it is.'

'I still think you're holding something back,' he demurred, 'something you'd rather not talk about.'

She sighed. 'It wouldn't do any good, Matt. Any problems I have, I have to work out by myself.'

He looked as though he could have said a lot more, but instead he ran a resigned hand round the back of his neck. As he lowered it he glanced at his watch. 'I guess you're right, Lee. If you don't love me and you've made up your mind, I suppose there's nothing more to be said.'

Feeling, she was sure, no better than he did, Lee followed him to the door. 'I hope we can still be friends?'

A faint smile broke the grimness of his features for the first time. Gently he bent and kissed her. 'Of course we can still be friends,' he said gruffly. 'If ever you need me, you know where to find me. I haven't stopped caring, you know.'

Lee wept after he had gone. She had hated hurting Matt. Breaking her engagement to him was one of the hardest things she had ever done, and possibly the most foolish! She had given up a fine man for—what? Another man who had no love or even respect for her.

Yet much as she tried to put Slade from her mind, she couldn't stop longing for him. She knew she had to see him again. Now that she was free, he might begin thinking differently about the future he wanted them to share. She loved him so deeply, she wasn't sure what she would do if the sole purpose of his recent manoeuvres had been merely to cause a break between herself and Matt.

It was five before Sandra got back. She had enjoyed the wedding, but it had been a hectic weekend and she was tired.

Lee made her a cup of tea. She had showered and used make-up to hide any visible signs of distress, and she must have made a good job of it, as Sandra didn't notice anything was wrong. 'Why didn't you stay a few more days?' she asked. Sandra's last patient didn't need her any more and she didn't take up her new post until the end of the week. 'It would have done you good.'

Sandra took her tea with scarcely a word of thanks. 'So you and Matt could have had the house to yourselves, don't you mean? I'm sorry if I've spoiled your fun.'

'Oh, Sandra!' After all her efforts, Lee felt the too ready tears scalding her eyes. 'I may as well tell you,' she rushed on, 'because you'd soon find out. Matt and I are no longer engaged.'

Sandra sat down abruptly, as if her legs had given way. 'Is this true?' she stared at Lee, her eyes doubtful.

'It's not something I'd lie about.'

Turning her cup around twice, Sandra dragged her eyes from Lee's strained face to look at it blindly. 'A lovers' quarrel, I suppose?'

'No,' Lee retorted sharply. 'And Matt and I have never been lovers, not in the way I think you mean. We didn't quarrel,' deliberately she continued to use the plural, 'we just discovered we didn't love each other and decided we would be wiser to part.'

Several different emotions chased over Sandra's usually stoical features. 'Well, I'm sorry,' she said slowly. 'And I shouldn't have implied what I did. I didn't really believe that either of you . . .'

Hastily Lee broke in, trying to end what was turning into an embarrassing conversation. 'I've suddenly remembered—Matt's father is ill and he said his mother would like to see you.'

'Me?' queried Sandra.

'Yes. He didn't say it was urgent. He just thinks she likes to talk to you, but he was going to ask you to go over this evening.'

Sandra looked at her shrewdly. 'But after you broke off your engagement he felt he couldn't stay.'

'I should think he forgot all about it,' Lee returned Sandra's stare levelly. 'We were both rather shaken, so he had some justification, but that has nothing to do with the message he left from his mother.'

Sandra brightened eagerly. 'No, I suppose not. Do you think I should still go? It's not late—if you wouldn't mind . . .?'

'Why should I?' Lee shrugged, then smiled. 'I'm sure you'll find Mrs Leland makes a better cup of tea than I do.'

'You're a dear!' Jumping up, Sandra hugged her impulsively, leaving Lee staring after her in bewilderment. Perhaps Sandra should try going to another wedding. Whatever had happened this weekend had certainly not done her any harm!

She wasn't surprised when Sandra spent the whole of the following days with the Lelands, and she tried to take advantage of having the house to herself by getting on with her writing. It made her anxious that her inspiration seemed to have dried up since Slade had returned. She found it increasingly difficult to concentrate on anything but him.

She had heard nothing from him since Sunday morning. All Monday she had expected the telephone to ring, but it had remained silent. On Tuesday, when Dulcie rang, commiserating over Lee's broken engagement and asking if she could 'pop round', Lee suddenly remembered an urgent appointment in Reading and put her off until the end of the week. She had had enough of Dulcie's curiosity on Sunday, when she had phoned to ask if Lee had heard anything more about her bike. What conclusions she had come to over her broken engagement, Lee dared not think. It puzzled her how the news had got so quickly about. Not Matt's doing, she was sure! But if Dulcie had heard, it must be even further afield, as Matt wasn't exactly unknown. If it was common knowledge then Slade wouldn't be unaware of it. It was more than likely that he had inveigled it out of Matt himself. This was why she was so frightened when Slade failed to call or get in touch. It seemed her worst fears had been realised.

Lee told herself that a trip out might provide the mental stimulus she was so clearly in need of. She refused to believe she was hoping to bump into Slade. She knew she was acting foolishly. Slade had achieved what he had set out to do, and hadn't she told him a dozen times that she wasn't interested in the kind of relationship he had to offer? Why should she complain if he'd been convinced she had meant everything she had said?

She had more pride than to call at his office and demand to see him, but the battle she fought with her pride proved so exhausting that she was wandering listlessly around a bookshop when Slade's mother came across her.

'It is Lee Moreau, isn't it?' Mrs Western cried eagerly.

Lee was startled, but couldn't prevent herself from looking pleased. 'Mrs Western! How nice to see you. Slade told me you were back.' She anticipated that she would be asked if she had seen him and felt it might be wiser to mention it straight away.

His mother smiled. 'He said he'd seen you, and I've been meaning to give you a ring.'

Had he mentioned it—or had his mother had to ask? 'I expect you've been busy settling in?'

'Yes, I have,' Mrs Western sighed eloquently. 'But Slade's away again.'

'Oh.'

'Hadn't you heard?'

Lee swallowed and shook her head, hoping she didn't look as suddenly shaken as she felt. She hadn't heard, but she might have known. Hollowly she murmured, 'He was always dashing off somewhere.'

'He expects to be gone a few weeks.'

Lee smiled, but with agony twisting inside her. This was Slade's answer to all her hopes and fears. It hadn't been necessary for him to come and see her or phone. Simply by disappearing he had told her all she had wanted to know. Hadn't wanted to know! she corrected herself bitterly.

'How does it feel to be living by the river again?' she asked with false brightness.

'I'm enjoying it,' Lydia smiled. 'I've always loved the Thames, of course. While Slade's away, why don't we take a trip down the river one day?'

'That would be lovely,' Lee agreed, hoping Mrs Western would forget about it. Slade wouldn't approve, even if he wanted nothing more to do with her.

'We're hoping to spend Christmas here,' Lydia smiled warmly at the girl she had never ceased to be extremely fond of. 'I've asked Slade to invite a few people, but before that we're planning a barbecue. It's going to be a huge affair; half Reading will be there. I hope you'll come, dear?'

'Someone's already mentioned it.' Lee didn't commit herself.

'Slade's not sure that he'll be back in time,' Lydia frowned. 'I've been hoping for years that he'll meet a nice girl and get married. I've a great desire for some grandchildren.'

Lee said nothing, and Lydia glanced at her sharply. 'Is it true what I've been hearing, that you're engaged?'

'Was,' Lee forced herself to speak lightly. 'To Matt Leland—a relation of yours, I believe?'

'His mother and I are third cousins.' Lydia looked as though she was sorting it out. 'We don't see a lot of each other. The last time I saw her she said that Matthew has a good practice.'

'Yes.'

'So what went wrong?'

'Wrong?' The bluntness of Mrs Leland's query took

Lee by surprise. For a moment she gazed at her blankly, then she flushed. 'Oh, my engagement, you mean? Well, nothing, I suppose. We just decided it had been a mistake.'

Lydia nodded understandingly, then was hailed by another friend. 'Don't forget our boat trip,' she said as she departed. 'I'll give you a ring.'

The week dragged on. For the first time in a long time, River Bend seemed too big and lonely for Lee. Matt picked Sandra up in the mornings and dropped her off again later in the day, but he didn't come in, and when Sandra began her new job the days seemed longer than ever. Nothing Lee did succeeded in taking her mind off Slade. Sometimes she thought of going off somewhere for a few months and seeing what an entirely new environment would do for her.

Her nerves were so strained that when Dulcie rang to ask if she would look after Trigg so she could spend the day with George, in London, she was so relieved she almost burst into tears. She would love to, she said, looking forward to his company, young as he was. She thought they might go for a picnic, but when Mrs Western called and, after hearing about Trigg, offered to take them both on the river, Lee was happy to accept.

Trigg was thrilled, and he and Mrs Western appeared to enjoy each other's company enormously. It was rather awkward trying to explain to Trigg that because Mrs Western was the mother of the man who had taken her bike, it might be better not to mention it, but he was so engrossed with the boat that he seemed to forget about everything else. Lee enjoyed herself, too, but the boat reminded her of Slade too much not to bring back painful memories.

Mrs Western was a proficient sailor and Lee had picked up a lot during the months she had lived abroad with Slade. They sailed past Reading and on towards Windsor. Trigg liked the locks best; he would have spent

the whole day negotiating them if he'd been allowed to.
He had a genius for getting wet, and Lee was glad she
was wearing a pair of serviceable jeans, because she
seemed to spend most of the day rescuing him.

After lunch, Lee told Mrs Western a little about him
when, exhausted from the morning's activities, he fell
asleep. She probably wouldn't have told her anything if
Mrs Western hadn't asked, but as Mrs Western was
obviously fond of children and was being extremely
kind, Lee couldn't see any harm in revealing a few
things about him which she was sure not even his
parents could object to. It seemed, however, that Trigg,
in the way of most children, had been revealing a few
things himself.

'He was telling me that he doesn't want to go away to
school,' Mrs Western mused. 'Do you think that's
because of his asthma?'

'Partly,' Lee frowned. 'I try not to say anything,
because if I had a family, I'm not sure I would
appreciate outsiders offering unasked-for and perhaps
unwanted advice on how to bring them up, but I've
grown so fond of Trigg that I'm afraid I have been
guilty of interfering sometimes.'

Lydia smiled sympathetically and not without
interest. 'What would you do if Trigg was your own
child?'

Lee flushed, wondering if she would ever have one of
her own. 'I think I'd forget about boarding school until
he was older. He's only eight and there's every chance
his health will improve. To send him away now, I feel,
would do more harm than good.'

'He might have benefited from a brother or sister,'
sighed Lydia. 'I've often thought Slade would have too,
especially when he was younger. He would have learned
to share and confide, not to keep everything to himself.'

Trigg woke and nothing more was said, but Lydia's
remarks lingered. Slade was possessive and didn't easily
share his thoughts, but Lee didn't believe this was a

trait that had much to do with being an only child. With Slade she had often felt he had learned not to trust, yet with a mother like Lydia, that didn't seem possible.

As the evenings were drawing in, they didn't stay late on the river. Lee was home in good time to cook dinner. Lydia asked her to dine with her, but she refused. Slade might not be pleased if he discovered she had spent the day with his mother, but he would be furious if she accepted an invitation to dine at his house while he was away. Trigg provided a convenient excuse as he was staying until the morning at River Bend and she wanted to get him into bed before he fell asleep again.

She reluctantly promised Lydia that she would think about coming to the barbecue, but when the night arrived she couldn't find sufficient courage. Pleading a headache, she told the others to go ahead, she would follow when she felt better. But she knew she wouldn't. On returning from Venice, Julia and Nigel had announced their engagement, which had distressed Julia when she had learned that Lee and Matt had broken theirs. Lee had glossed over it, telling her much the same story as she had told Sandra, but she was aware that Julia wasn't as easily deceived. Despite Lee's protestations, Julia suspected her heart was breaking. It might be, Lee thought heavily, but Matt wasn't responsible.

Left on her own, she let herself quietly out of the house and wandered through the fields to the river. After a while she sat down in one of her favourite spots under some huge willow trees. The sound of the gently rippling water soothed her, along with the unobtrusive sounds of the night. Through the dipping branches of the willows she noticed a water-vole plunge from the bank and disappear into its hole, while above her head an owl hooted softly in the trees. Lee tried to spot its exact location, but it was too well hidden from sight.

Being well acquainted with the small creatures of the river bank, she knew no fear, but the crunch of footsteps on some dying foliage startled her. Suddenly apprehensive, she scrambled to her feet and turned, to find Slade approaching her. It was dusk, but there was no mistaking his tall, commanding figure. Unconsciously she shivered. How many times over the past weeks had she longed for such a moment, yet now it was here she almost wished she could disappear like the water-vole.

'Lee?' His voice reached her before he did, playing on her already heightened senses.

'Slade?' She tried to hide how shaken she felt. 'You're the last person I expected to see.'

'Why?' He stopped beside her, viewing her startled expression with an indulgent smile.

As his mouth quirked with amusement, his impregnable confidence made her suddenly angry. Her blue eyes flashed. 'You haven't been here for three weeks and you ask me that!'

'Business kept me away,' he muttered, his glance becoming as intent as her own as he towered above her.

Lee's pulses raced, refusing to be unmoved by him. He was wearing dark jeans which clung to his powerful thighs, blatantly outlining his aggressive masculinity. The black shirt moulding his broad shoulders lay open at the neck, revealing the strength of his throat and the dark shading of hair on his chest. 'You didn't ring.' There was reproach in her voice.

'Did you expect me to?'

'After our last conversation,' she said, more sharply, 'I thought you might.'

'I've been busy,' he replied absently.

He was staring at her oddly, his eyes fixed on her face. He seemed to be drinking her in. Lee had the strange feeling that his mind was only half on what he was saying. His close glance went over her quickly, then slowed, like that of a hungry man confronted by a wonderful feast and bent on savouring every delicious morsel of it. Up from her slender body, his gaze lingered on high cheekbones, the thick, dark lashes framing wide-set eyes. Her face had a delicate, exotic quality which combined with a willowy yet voluptuous figure gave her a haunting beauty that Slade was never able to forget for long. She dimmed every other woman's appeal for him and, as always, he resented it, especially when, as though amused by his resistance, his own body hardened against his wishes.

'You can't have been that busy!' she retorted.

'No,' he agreed, frustration edging the glint of anger from his eyes. 'You're quite right, I could have made time, and God knows there were plenty of times when I wanted to speak to you, but I knew there was only one thing you would want to talk about.'

'Matt.'

'I had no particular wish to hear how he'd reacted after you told him you couldn't marry him. I thought I'd give you time to forget.'

A terrible coldness invaded her that he could be so utterly callous. The nerves in her stomach might knot at the sight of him, her heart race, but she would be very foolish to have anything more to do with him. 'How do you know I'm not still engaged to Matt?' she cried recklessly.

'I have my spies,' he smiled smugly. 'And my mother told me—and,' he caught her hand, bringing her fingers, in a gesture she knew so well, to his lips, 'you aren't wearing his ring.'

Was he pleased because she was free again or only because he'd got his own way? 'I should never have given Matt up,' she fretted, her fingers curling against the sensation shooting up her arm from Slade's lingering lips.

He released her hand with a cruel twist. 'Let's forget Matt. Have you missed me?'

She grabbed the chance of tit for tat. 'I've been busy.'

He saw no humour in her subtle revenge, his eyes darkened as he took his. 'I might have known you wouldn't be honest.'

Lee's voice shook with rage. 'If I told you how much I missed you, where would that get me?'

Throwing back his head, he laughed dryly, 'A lot closer than your temper!' He let go of her hand and lifted his arms. 'Come here.'

Not ready yet to be so acquiescent, she tried to retreat, but as their eyes met and his desire was instantly communicated, she also recognised the power he had over her. When his hands closed over her shoulders, his touch weakened her control and she couldn't fight it. Liquid fire began spreading to every part of her body, rendering her helpless. Aware of the compelling danger, she tried to stiffen her vacillating senses. Slade knew about Matt and hadn't even the decency to pretend he was sorry! It annoyed her that he could interfere so ruthlessly in other people's lives and set it behind him so easily. Everything about him should be a warning, so why didn't she have the sense to take proper precautions?

He didn't try to hold her. She had withdrawn, but he sensed her fluctuating inclinations as expertly as he read weather signs at sea. When she frowned as he released her, unable to hide a contrary dismay, his appealing smile was a masterpiece of triumph delayed. 'Why won't you say you've missed me?'

'Why did you come?' she countered, unsteadily, feeling that if she answered him she might be completely lost.

'There's a party you're invited to, remember?'

She frowned as he watched her intently. 'I wasn't going.'

'But you are now, with me.'

She smiled, unable to restrain a sudden bubbling happiness. That Slade had come to accompany her to one of his mother's parties must mean something. She heard his quick intake of breath at the sheer loveliness of her face when she smiled. It seemed to confirm what she had just been thinking, and she made no further attempt to evade him as he drew her close again. The raw sexuality he exuded was an almost tangible force that reached out and captured her with its very intensity, making her realise the futility of continuing to oppose him.

He held her firmly with one hand while the fingers of his other laced through her hair. As his mouth lowered to meet hers she saw something in his eyes that tore down the barricade she had erected round her heart. Wordlessly she returned his kiss, and everything faded; the river, the softly rustling trees along its bank, the whispering wind. Slade's closeness was like a balm to the loneliness she had suffered over the past weeks. As he filled her with warmth she let the pain flow out of her and welcomed it rapturously. When his arms tightened and his kiss deepened, she matched him in ardency.

The passion of his kiss was so overwhelming that she couldn't immediately pull herself together when he raised his head. 'Now tell me you haven't missed me,' he said.

'I have,' she confessed at last, wondering why he was so insistent. He had so much self-confidence, didn't he take it for granted that she had missed him?

'Why wouldn't you say so straight away?' he demanded, 'You'd like me to believe you care for me, yet you're always reluctant to show it.'

'Perhaps I'm frightened,' she sighed, recognising her own vulnerability if he didn't.

'I'd never do anything to harm you,' he said, refusing to look under the surface of her words. 'Lee,' his voice thickened, 'I want you.'

'Yes,' her smile was tremulous, her hand trembled as she brought it from behind his neck and played with a button on his shirt.

He captured her hand and stared at her, his breathing deepening, his eyes black. 'You're sure?'

She hesitated, but he captured her mouth again and she was lost. 'Come back to the house,' he said hoarsely, 'I've been through hell without you.'

Lee tried to think clearly. 'I'll have to go back to change. Julia and Sandra dressed up.'

'Yes,' he muttered, but didn't move.

She felt tremors ripping through him, from his taut stomach to his muscular thighs, and her desire for him flamed to life, like an explosion of fireworks. All her resolutions to keep him at a distance faded. He had stopped talking and held her as though she was all he ever wanted. His arms locked about her as though he would never let her go, and her arms stole round his neck and drew his head towards hers.

# CHAPTER SEVEN

SLADE understood her silent plea only too well. Their mouths met and joined in a searing alliance that blazed a fiery streak right through her. She reached on her toes to get even closer to him than his straining arms allowed. She had never experienced such a volume of feeling from a single kiss. They seemed to be merging as a single unit of fire and flame and intense need.

When Slade ended the kiss he was breathing hard and the hand he placed under her chin, unsteady. Silence hung heavily between them as they gazed into each other's eyes, trying to read behind their individual masks.

'Why can't you be honest with me, Lee?' he asked, his voice tight and hard. 'You have some feelings for me, yet you delight in denying them. You treat me like a new date instead of someone you know intimately.'

Lee took a deep breath, being even less adept at reading his thoughts than he was of hers. Did it really matter to him whether she cared for him or not? He always told her he didn't know how he felt, so why was the way she felt important to him? She shook her head uncertainly and evaded his hand to rest her cheek on his chest. The disturbed beat of his heart surprised her and set her own off at a similar speed.

'We have no time to talk now,' she protested evasively.

'Talking won't be necessary if you're prepared to be sensible.'

He took her face in his steely hands and slowly lowered his mouth to open hers. He was rapidly tearing down all her defences, but for the moment she was helpless to stop him.

'The barbecue?' she reminded him, without stirring. She wanted to go to the barbecue now, she knew a wild joy that he wanted to take her, but she found it difficult to move.

He stared down at her. 'It can wait. The grass is dry.' He pressed her against him.

She felt his need matching her own and her blood surged in instant response. Lifting heavy lashes, she met his eyes. His were wild and strange. The astute, in-control-of-everything business man had gone, leaving a susceptible human being. He wanted her and in this way, at least, she was important to him.

A primitive longing welled up inside Lee, so strong that she offered no resistance when Slade lowered her to the soft grass under the trees.

'You're my woman,' he growled.

His words washed over her softly. If only she was, in every way! He made such a statement, possibly to rule out any further opposition. He didn't seem to realise she needed a sense of security.

Yet how could she argue with him when her senses were reeling and he was holding her so closely, as though he never intended letting her go? His hands travelled over every inch of her, weaving a spell with every light, tormenting stroke. All she could manage was strangled gasps as passion spiralled and threatened to consume her. Her arms wound round his neck as she met the savage demand of his kisses like an acceptance of all he was saying, without further demur.

She quaked as he swiftly undressed them and her slender frame met the hard planes of his naked body. His husky whispers proclaiming her beauty, the satiny feel of her skin, soon thickened unintelligibly, and the sheer intensity of his throbbing desire swept her into a realm of the senses where nothing else existed but his hands, mouth and voice. The feelings she had denied for so long rose to swamp any lingering trace of common sense. Their surroundings faded as he made passionate love to her, until eventually everything else was blotted out.

Later, Lee heard the leaves rustle above her head, but her eyes were focussed dreamily on Slade's face. In the pale glow of light from the rising moon she could see the fine film of sweat still on his brow as he lay down beside her. His strong body was relaxed against her and her eyes wandered until his sheer male magnificence began stirring a sharp awareness in her again, making her conscious of what she was doing.

As she flushed, he smiled lazily and kissed her as he read her mind. 'Don't worry, I feel the same way.'

'We shouldn't.'

'No?' he teased, then softly smoothed the tangled hair from off her damp forehead. 'You don't know how much I've longed to have you in my arms. I don't want to let you go.'

Lee was willing to believe him. His lovemaking had been so intense, it convinced her he hadn't been amusing himself with other women while he'd been away. Her colour deepened when she thought of the heights they had reached and she pulled the shirt he had wrapped protectively round her closer, as though to hide her confusion.

'I wanted to go slowly,' he told her, his eyes darkening, 'but I wanted you so badly. Do you have any idea what you do to me, Lee? I've been aching for you.'

She curled nearer, her fingers twisting in the fine matt of hair on his chest. He trembled, and the swiftness of his reaction thrilled her afresh. Did that mean he was beginning to love her? Hope soared. He had revealed that while he had been away she had never been far from his thoughts. Surely that must mean something?

He eased himself up a little and made her look at him, as if it was important that he saw her expression. Staring into her eyes, he commanded, 'Tell me you welcome me back.'

Lee sighed. 'Must we return to—that——'

His hurt bewilderment was reminiscent of a small boy's, but she wished he hadn't had a small boy's perseverance. 'When a man's important to a girl it usually shows.'

Lee marvelled, after the response she had just shown, that such a minor detail as this still bothered him. 'I think our relationship has made me cautious,' she replied honestly. 'I've been lonely . . .'

'You won't be again,' he cut in.

What exactly did that mean?

'Trust me, Lee.'

She wanted to. She loved him so much, she couldn't bear to think he would ever let her down, but she feared they weren't thinking along the same lines.

Slade nuzzled her neck, feeling the strain of the past weeks seep out of him. 'We have a party to go to.'

She heard him, but made no attempt to get up. His arms were locked around her, he didn't seem in a hurry to go anywhere, and she decided weakly to wait until he made the first move. Tentatively, she let her hand wander further, revelling in the luxury of having him with her again.

His dark eyes narrowed on her with a passionate intensity she hadn't encountered before and she couldn't look away. Instead she absorbed him into the depth of her, letting him become part of her. He lifted the shirt covering her and she basked in his rapt expression which sent her pulses hammering through her veins. She found herself dissolving under it and felt more helpless now than ever before. Simply by looking at her, it seemed, Slade could trap her in a whirlwind.

'You're beautiful, Lee,' his burning glance riveted on her high breasts and narrow waist, long, slender legs. 'You're a temptress, a witch, and I can't get enough of you.'

His fingers trembled as he traced the curves of her tender lips and a disturbing sensuality entered his face as he threaded his hand through the silken length of her hair, holding her head firmly. His mouth descended slowly towards hers, gently exploring, then boldly investigating the inner recesses of her parted lips. His kisses deepened as he lowered himself over the throbbing fullness of her breasts, only allowing himself room to test the hardening response of her betraying nipples with his hand.

'I want you again,' he groaned.

He knew she wanted him, so why deny it? As his kisses branded her with the stamp of his possession, she became less able to fight him. With each kiss she became more and more drugged, with every touch her breathing more laboured. When his mouth followed his fingers to her breast, she resisted no longer. She became lost to everything but her own desire.

'I need you, I love you,' she entreated hoarsely.

His mouth, which had been feathering her cheek, moved in a blazing path to her lips. His kisses stopped taunting and became savagely intense. He was either accepting or rejecting what she had said. Either way, he was allowing a savage physical reaction to blot out his thoughts. She was almost crushed by his strength before the onslaught of his mouth gentled and he exercised considerable restraint.

Nevertheless, he went on kissing her, though this time he slowed to let them savour more thoroughly the ever rising volume of feeling between them. His hands again travelled over every part of her, coming to rest between her thighs. Here, the exquisite ache at the bottom of her stomach demanded he should possess her immediately, but this time he made her wait. He appeared oblivious of her silent urges as he seemed bent on arousing her to the point of no return. Through the heated cloud of her mind, Lee was drunkenly amazed that he could hold out so long. As he held her tightly she was aware of his overwhelming desire.

Lee writhed and twisted under the sweet torment he

was forcing her to endure. Her fingernails dug into the muscled contours of his back in an urgent attempt to force him to satisfy the clamouring of her senses which were now screaming for release. Finally, as she cried out his name, he became wholly part of her, moving slowly and deeply, letting their combined and devastating sensuality carry them to the higher pinnacles they seemed to reach every time. Lee's whimpers of ecstasy were drowned by his groans of passionate satisfaction until at last, as if on wings, they both soared heavenwards, to find total completion together.

Afterwards he kissed her and lifted her reluctantly to her feet. 'Come on,' he teased gently, steadying her as she swayed. 'We can still make the party if we hurry. I'll help you change.'

'I'll make it quicker on my own,' she said dryly, but her fingers trembled as she zipped up her jeans.

'I'd better approve what you're wearing,' Slade insisted possessively as they began walking back to the house. 'Seeing you're going to be my partner.'

She was so pleased about this that she stifled further objections as he followed her upstairs. She even allowed him to select a dress, as he had often done, with unerring taste when they had lived together. She hadn't the selection now that she had had then, but he choose a strappy, ankle-length silk in dazzling shades of blue and green which made her look, he told her later, like some exotic bird of paradise.

'Don't take all night,' he ordered, so presumptuously that she might have thrown a pillow at him if he hadn't guessed her intention and his eyes warned her where that could lead! Instead, she smiled at him and contented herself with retreating to the bathroom and bolting the door. Her new docility appeared to please him, and she had no wish to disturb his present mood. He hadn't suggested they might live together again and the hope in her heart that had been wilting suddenly began to bloom.

She had no conscience over turning herself into the vision of loveliness Slade had been used to seeing in New York and Paris. No regret, either, for the way his breath caught audibly in his throat as she emerged from the bathroom, a radiantly beautiful woman yet looking not a day over eighteen.

'My God, Lee!' He was lounging in a chair, waiting impatiently, and when she entered he sprang to his feet. 'You look wonderful! I'm going to have a job fending other men off.'

Lee smiled but retreated as he walked towards her, an unmistakable smouldering in his eyes. Tossing back her beautiful mane of gleaming hair, she slanted a teasing glance at him through ridiculously long lashes. 'I've made up my mind to stun everyone tonight, and I won't be side-tracked again.'

'Not even for . . .?' His glance went meaningly to the bed.

'No,' she said firmly, but her pulse began racing with renewed excitement as she saw colour creeping under his skin and she knew they might never get anywhere unless she insisted.

The telephone rang, settling the silent battle between them. 'Yes?' Lee answered breathlessly.

'Lee?' Julia exclaimed, 'You don't sound yourself. Are you all right?'

'Yes,' Lee repeated, shaking her head at Slade as he asked by gestures who it was. 'I'm coming to the party—I'm on my way.'

'We are,' said Slade.

'Are you talking to someone?' Julia sounded puzzled.

'The cat. See you in a few minutes.' Lee replaced the receiver quickly.

'You haven't a cat,' frowned Slade, as she explained who it was.

'You remind me of a big one,' she retorted sharply. 'And if you don't like the comparison, it was your own fault for interrupting. She heard you talking and I had to say something.'

'Try the truth next time,' he advised dryly, with no obvious compunction as her cheeks went scarlet at the very thought.

The party was well under way when they arrived. To Lee's surprise, Slade drove round the back of the house. 'Like you, I have to change,' he smiled. 'Go in the front and find your friends. I'll join you later.'

He was gone before she could protest, leaving Lee to wander somewhat unhappily in the direction he had indicated. He had said he was taking her to the party, but who would get that impression when she went in alone? Was that what he had intended? Again she was cruelly reminded of how impossible it was to tell what Slade was thinking. An hour ago she had believed the future looked promising. Now she wasn't so sure again.

Fortunately she spotted Julia and Nigel as soon as she walked through the front door. They had been looking out for her and didn't mind when she joined them. Julia glanced behind Lee, as if she expected to see someone accompanying her, and, on realising she was alone, gave her a strange look.

Lee pretended not to see. 'There's quite a crowd,' she observed.

'A lot here,' Nigel agreed. He smiled at both girls, his gaze lingering teasingly on his beloved. 'Julia didn't know where to begin. There's dancing outside and in and a buffet or a barbecue, whatever takes your fancy, and that's just for starters!'

'It's a wonderful house,' said Julia in a kind of hushed voice. 'If I were the Westerns, I don't think I could bear to leave it. I'm glad you were able to come, Lee. I feared you might be going down with something. Have you been here before?'

'Once or twice. I know Mrs Western.'

'Yes, of course you must,' exclaimed Julia. 'Isn't Matt related . . .? Oh, sorry!' her gentle eyes filled with self-impatience, 'I really do have a knack of putting my foot in it, don't I? That's why you didn't want to come.'

'Nothing of the sort,' Lee denied crisply. 'If that had been the case I wouldn't have changed my mind, would I? Neither Matt or I are suffering from broken hearts.'

At that moment Matt appeared with a laughing Sandra hanging on his arm. Matt looked so content that Lee was suddenly sure she was speaking the truth. It was the first time he and Lee had met since she had ended their engagement, but he didn't seem like a man with a broken heart. She actually felt nonplussed by the way he seemed to be enjoying himself with Sandra.

Where was Slade? Lee wasn't enjoying the pitying glances she was receiving and wished he would rescue her. She couldn't see him anywhere. Surely he'd had enough time to change twice over? When she spotted him talking to a group of people, she regretted having wondered. He wasn't exactly rushing to her side, and her heart began its familiar aching.

'There's Slade over there!' exclaimed Matt. 'Everybody's been wondering where he'd got to. I was beginning to think he wasn't coming.'

'He's been away three weeks,' Nigel told Lee, unaware that she had counted every hour.

Numbly she nodded. Ought she to pretend she hadn't known? A moment later Slade was behind her, relieving her of making the decision. She heard him asking in the manner of a genial host, 'Everyone enjoying themselves?'

There was a general murmur of assent and Julia and Sandra stared at him curiously. Matt introduced the girls briefly, then said carefully, 'I believe you've already met Lee?'

'Yes.' To Lee's surprise, just as she was beginning to feel abandoned, Slade slipped a proprietorial arm around her. 'We go back a long time, don't we, Lee?'

She glanced at him quickly, over her shoulder. He was dressed formally in a dark jacket and tie and was so handsome that she returned his smile involuntarily, but she wished he hadn't phrased his remark quite so blatantly. She didn't have to see the sudden suspicion in Matt's eyes to know it was there. Nigel was staring too, though his glance was trained more on the arm Slade had around her waist.

'I used to work for Mrs Western,' she said quickly.

Slade grinned and pulled her closer. 'My mother thought the world of her, and so did I.'

Sandra nudged Matt, sharing his suspicious glance, and Lee felt a hint of disquiet. What was Slade thinking about? Was he playing one of his devious games, or was he trying to establish their former friendship so that any announcement they might make wouldn't cause too much surprise? Settling on the latter, for her own peace of mind, she smiled at him radiantly again when he asked her to come with him for a drink.

Still with his arm round her, they wandered outside to the bar, which had been set up in a huge marquee. They attracted attention even in that short distance, and though she was loath to, Lee wriggled away from him. Until she was sure of Slade's motives, she didn't want to risk having people feeling sorry for her later.

He raised a mocking brow as she put space between them. 'That's not very friendly.'

'But wiser.'

His demoniacal brow didn't lower. 'Since when have you been noted for your wisdom, my darling?'

His words were so taunting she shivered. 'You don't have to rub it in. As far as you're concerned, I don't think I have any.'

She accepted a Martini. Without consulting her, Slade had asked the barman to mix it just as she liked it. While she thanked him, she was sure she wasn't imagining the slight frost in his manner. He had asked her to trust him and sensed that she still didn't.

'Where's your mother?' As he threw back a whisky, Lee glanced around, trying to spot her.

'You'd hardly find her in here.'

'I know!' she resented his dryness, 'but I haven't said hello yet.'

'You spent the day with her on the river. Surely that was enough?'

His voice had cooled. Lee sensed his displeasure, which did nothing to dispel the things bothering her. 'Trigg Mansfield was with us. I had him for the day.'

'While his charming parents were out enjoying themselves?'

Lee was surprised to find herself defending them stiffly. 'George goes to London every day, but Dulcie rarely goes with him, and everyone needs to get away sometimes. There are so few people Dulcie feels she can ask to look after Trigg. Not many are keen to have him for fear of his asthma.'

'Ah, yes,' shrugged Slade, 'I forgot about the asthma.'

'Most people would rather forget about it!' she said angrily.

'I'm sure not intentionally.' Frowning, he touched her heated cheek. 'Why so mad?'

'I only get mad when people are indifferent to what's going on about them.'

'You think I am?' He sounded hurt.

'Unless it suits you.'

'I never forget about you, do I?'

His taunting tone incensed her. 'You find ways of keeping tabs on me, but I can't feel flattered.'

Slade laughed, his eyes suddenly amused. 'Lee, my love, we shouldn't be fighting this evening, of all evenings, should we?'

Lee coloured enchantingly at the intimate note in his voice, instantly diverted. 'What—what's so special about this one?' she faltered, her face suddenly glowing. Let him tell me he wants to marry me, she prayed. It wouldn't matter if he didn't love her as

much as she loved him. She couldn't bear the thought
of any other kind of relationship now. She wanted to
be his wife!

A wary expression on his handsome face, Slade said
smoothly, 'Doesn't it seem a special night to you? This
is no ordinary party, and you can't have forgotten the
events leading up to it. I'll never be able to sit on a river
bank and think only about the scenery again.'

Lee thought of Paris, the Seine. He hadn't thought
only of the scenery then. Helplessly she sighed. If he
had read her mind, that didn't prove he was putting her
off deliberately. He could hardly propose to her now,
with so many people around. He must be thinking of it,
though, or he wouldn't be looking at her the way he
was doing? Deciding to do nothing to dampen his
ardour, she smiled at him and enjoyed hearing his
breath catch.

His face darkened as their eyes met. 'For God's sake,
Lee,' he said thickly, 'don't flutter your lashes at me
here, unless you're prepared to take the consequences,
which could be a lot more embarrassing for you than
me.'

Lee flushed and bristled. 'You wouldn't dare!'

'Even a kiss would be enough to set tongues wagging
for a month.'

As her eyes widened, he must have felt she was
sufficiently punished, for he squeezed her hand
comfortingly. 'Matt doesn't seem to be suffering too
badly, though he definitely didn't like my arm around
you.'

'You aren't very tactful, are you?' she sighed.

'Cruel to be kind,' he retorted indifferently.

'I think he's discovering a fondness for Sandra.' If
there was a rueful note in her voice, Lee had no idea it
was there, but there was no mistaking Slade's tight-
lipped anger.

'Regretting him already, are we?'

She could have started another minor battle, with

some justification, but she was learning restraint. Slade and she couldn't be forever at loggerheads. Yet she couldn't stop the impulsive remark that leapt to her lips. 'The only thing I ever regret is you!'

His anger was replaced by a silky iciness which scared her even more. 'You may feel you regret the past, Lee, but when you're older . . .'

'I'm older now,' she cut in.

'And I like you better,' a little warmth returned to his eyes. 'Before, you worried me too much. Now you're more mature, you can't pretend not to know what you're doing, and I find you infinitely more satisfying.'

Would she ever be able to read between the lines of what he was saying? She might be older, but she was in no way more competent in that respect. Lee gazed at him in confusion, not knowing what to think.

'Are you hungry yet?' he asked, a more tolerant gleam in his eye when she was obviously silenced by his last statement.

'No, not yet.' A few minutes ago she had been, but now her appetite seemed strangely depleted.

Taking her half full glass, he set it aside. 'As you're neither hungry nor apparently thirsty, let's dance.'

Wishing she had declared she was ravenous, Lee allowed herself to be guided outside again. There were people everywhere, the dance floor was crowded and Slade had to hold her very close for her own protection. Or so he said. Somehow, she wasn't sure that she wanted to be in his arms, but as soon as they closed around her, she melted into them, as always feeling part of him when he was so near.

They circled the floor, oblivious to their surroundings, for several dances until Slade heaved a rueful sigh. 'If Lydia spends much longer trying to attract my attention unobtrusively, she's going to get in difficulties. I'd better go and see what she wants.'

Lee felt guilty. 'You're neglecting your duties.'

'I suppose I am,' he admitted. 'You can come and share the blame.'

Lydia Western had a charming smile for Lee but a more reproachful one for her son. 'I've lost count of the people asking to speak to you, Slade, wondering where you are.'

'I haven't been hiding,' he said dryly, 'but I'll circulate for half an hour, if you like, before Lee and I eat.' He added a postscript, 'Don't let Lee out of your sight.'

'Is he frightened someone's going to run away with you?' Lydia sounded amused, but her eyes were thoughtful as they followed her son before she turned back to Lee. 'You two seem—friendlier,' she remarked tentatively.

'Yes,' Lee replied cautiously. Mrs Western must remember the antagonism which had existed between them. It surprised Lee that she did, after so long.

Lydia sighed and asked what she thought of the party.

Lee congratulated her warmly and with sincere admiration for such a superb feat of organisation. 'I don't know how you've managed it.'

'Ann Bowie is with me,' replied Lydia. 'I meant to mention it when we were on the river. She's been an enormous help.'

Lee felt suddenly cold. The Bowies had been the cause of the trouble between herself and Slade. 'She had a son, hasn't she?' she asked nervously.

'Ray—yes,' Mrs Western frowned. 'He went abroad a few years ago, Slade found him a job, but Ann still worries over him.'

'I thought Slade didn't like him?' Lee exclaimed.

'I think he didn't approve of the life the boy was leading, but Slade's bark is often worse than his bite. He certainly helped Ray a lot, once the boy was willing to listen to him.'

They chatted for a while, relaxed as they always were

in each other's company and finding plenty to talk about. When Slade returned, his mother released Lee reluctantly. 'If I don't get another chance to speak to you, dear, I'll give you a ring soon and perhaps you'll come to dinner.'

'Ignore that,' Slade snapped tersely, almost dragging Lee towards the buffet.

'Why?' she asked tightly, while her heart sank.

'You won't have time.'

She couldn't be sure that he had hesitated before he replied, or why she found his reply somewhat less than reassuring.

Julia and Sandra were in the buffet with Nigel and Matt dancing attendance. 'We could have eaten at the barbecue,' Slade's glance followed hers across the room, 'but I knew your friends were here. Shall we join them?'

Lee could have sworn that an hour ago he had intended carrying a trayful of food from the barbecue to some shadowed corner of the grounds, where they could be alone. Obviously he had changed his mind. Stifling a sigh of regret, she nodded.

He was charming to Julia and Sandra, and Lee wasn't surprised that they were soon captivated. Nigel, after seeming slightly overwhelmed by Slade's presence, soon joined in the conversation, making them all laugh with his dry humour which helped to draw attention from the increasingly speculative glances Matt was throwing in their direction.

They finished a delectable feast just in time to see the fireworks display. 'Something gave me an enormous appetite this evening,' Slade teased as the first rocket went up. 'Do you remember our three o'clock in the morning feasts?' he whispered in her ear.

She flushed deeply and pretended to be absorbed by the explosion of multi-coloured stars in the sky, but he put a hand to her cheek and gave a satisfied chuckle at the heat he found there.

'I don't know where Mother gets all her ideas from,' Slade mused indulgently when the display was over and they wandered in the gardens.

'Or her energy.'

Slade frowned. 'She hasn't as much of that as she used to have, though she wouldn't admit it. I've told her that after this she must take things easy.'

'She was saying she could do with another secretary,' Lee remarked without thinking. 'I was surprised when she said she's never had one, since me.'

'Don't you dare accept if she asks you again,' he commanded sharply. 'I've other plans for you.'

Lee wondered what they were. If Slade asked her to marry him, as his wife, he surely wouldn't object if she helped his mother occasionally.

He paused beside a tinkling fountain set in a wide pool of moon-spangled water. With green lawns, herbaceous borders, conifers and broad-leafed trees for a background, the whole effect was incredibly lovely. Lee thought the coloured lights in the trees gave an exotic, Japanese effect. She had once visited Japan and never forgotten the beauty of their gardens.

Slade bent his head and kissed her lightly when she finished enthusing. 'You're the most beautiful thing around here. There isn't a man this evening who's not wishing he were in my shoes.'

She smiled and kissed him back, reluctant to even think of other men, content to revel in the close sense of companionship she felt between them as they wandered on.

After a while, Slade said wryly, 'I'm going to have to tear myself away for another spell of duty, but after that we can leave.'

Back in the house, Lee told him she would look for Julia and Sandra, but before she could find them she was waylaid by other friends, and then a man whom she knew vaguely asked her to dance. From that moment she was on the floor continually. At one time, there were actually several young men queuing up to dance with her.

It was as she finished dancing with one of them that someone carrying a brightly coloured drink bumped into her, spilling most of it over her. Amidst a flurry of embarrassed apologies, someone advised Lee to try and find some place to rinse as much of the cocktail out of her dress as she could, before it left a stain.

Thinking it might be the best thing to do, with some of her skirt sticking to her like glue, Lee hurried upstairs. Remembering where the bathrooms were, she ran past the first, which someone was using, into the second. She bolted the door as she decided it would be easier to remove the stain if she took her dress off, but she needn't have bothered, for the bathroom was well along the corridor, and no one else came.

The operation completed successfully, Less hastily tidied herself, and she hadn't taken more than two steps back along the corridor when Slade pounced on her.

'Where the devil have you been?' he snapped.

Lee shrank from the black rage in his eyes, but before she could defend herself he added furiously, 'Not content to flirt with every man who comes near you, you start poking around up here!'

'I wasn't flirting with other men,' she choked, feeling incredibly hurt. 'You shouldn't misconstrue being ordinarily pleasant . . .'

'Pleasant!' his mouth twisted in a sneer. 'You were draped all over the last fool you danced with. Don't forget, I remember how you used to be.'

'I was young,' she gasped, unable to associate this glowering stranger with the man she had been so close to all evening. 'And I never did more than smile at anyone in the old days, I suppose as a kind of experiment. You should know just how far I didn't go!' she reminded him bitterly.

That didn't stop him abusing her. 'You had all the inclinations, though. If I hadn't stepped in when I did you would have gone off with the next man who asked you. Don't try and tell me that all that passion could have been locked up indefinitely!'

Feeling like hitting him, she shouted, 'You forced me to go with you, and now you can only resort to insults!'

'I took you away for your own good, but your dishonest tendencies seemingly haven't been cured. I warned you what could happen if you were caught again, but you can't learn, can you? Most of my mother's jewellery is safely locked away, but you could probably find something if you looked hard enough.'

'You're despicable!' she cried, when a clatter at the other far end of the corridor spun them both around sharply.

There was no one there. Their argument briefly forgotten, Slade went to investigate, but found nothing. 'The wind must have rocked something,' he said. 'There's a window open.'

Lee felt too wounded to give it a second thought. Slade still distrusted her. She must have been crazy to imagine he intended marrying her. Her eyes filled with tears which, in turn, filled the man watching her with a rough kind of remorse. With a muffled exclamation, he gathered her abruptly to him.

'Oh, Lee!' he groaned. 'Maybe the girl you are, I've helped to make. I certainly don't seem to have been a good influence, but let's not quarrel over it.'

'Someone spilt something on my dress,' she sobbed. 'I came up here to wash it out. That's all I've been doing, I promise you.'

He smoothed her head against his chest, searching for a handkerchief. 'I'm sorry, Lee,' he murmured as he dried her eyes, but she could tell he wasn't sure what to believe. 'Let's forget about it,' he repeated. 'The party's nearly over, I think we can safely leave. We still have things to settle, and Lydia's quite capable of saying goodbye to the last of the guests.'

# CHAPTER EIGHT

By the time she was seated in his car, Lee felt considerably better. She had shown Slade the stained damp patch on her dress and he had suddenly recalled hearing snatches of talk about the incident downstairs. He had apologised so anxiously that Lee had eventually forgiven him, and the hurt that still lingered had been with her for so many years that she had learned somehow to live with it.

Slade glanced at her as she sat beside him, looking small and vulnerable. He didn't really believe she had been going to steal anything. He didn't altogether trust her, but his instincts had convinced him, long ago, that she wasn't a thief. Certain facts remained that couldn't be easily explained, but, this evening, it had been seeing her laughing so happily with other men that had aroused an ungovernable rage within him. There had been some talk flying around about an accident with some wine, but when he couldn't see Lee he had been so sure she had disappeared into the gardens with her last partner that he hadn't stopped to think. He had searched the grounds, and his temper had reached a dangerously high level before he had found her upstairs. It had been too late to control himself, and he had accused her of other things in order to hide his rampant and, as it had turned out, unjustifiable jealousy which, at all costs, she must never suspect. She aroused in him too many feelings he didn't understand and was determined to ignore. Certainly he didn't want Lee, with her deplorable feminine intuition, having a field-day dissecting his emotions. He felt bad enough as things were.

When he made no immediate attempt to start the car,

but after a first swift glance at her lapsed into a forbidding silence, Lee became tense again. She didn't want to start examining the underlying issues of Slade's attack on her, because she knew it could only stem from one thing, a fundamental distrust that had never died. And if she had ever thought the time had come to explain what had really happened, that night in his mother's bedroom so many years ago, having learned that Ann Bowie was still with his mother and her son Ray was now working for him, her hands seemed tied more than ever. How could she take her own happiness at the expense of others, especially as there was no guarantee that if Slade knew the truth it would make any difference?

'I could have gone home with Julia and Nigel,' she said unevenly, when Slade's silence and her own thoughts grew more than she could bear.

'No!' He turned to her quickly, catching her hand and carrying it to his lips as he gathered her suddenly into his arms. He looked pale, even in the dim light, though she just caught a brief glimpse of his face before he laid his hard cheek against hers. For a while he just held her, twisting his lean body so he didn't hurt her but as if it was imperative that she was close to him. She felt the hard strength of his legs pressing against her slighter limbs and, as her whole being began to throb, she wondered helplessly how he could draw such an overwhelming response from her, merely by holding her like this.

'Sweetheart!' he groaned. 'I realise I've made a hash of what promised to be a perfect evening, but it's going to kill me if you won't forgive me, really forgive me, I mean. I was scared when I couldn't find you. I feared . . .'

When he clamped down on his next words, Lee believed it was because of a reluctance to speak of his distrust again. But because the hand that lightly caressed her shook slightly, she excused him. He was usually so self-assured that even a small hint of vulnerability made her heart swell with love for him, blotting out all her resentment. Wasn't she more to blame than he was for the doubts he still harboured, for hadn't he had only the evidence of his own eyes?

Not trying to hide her love, she turned her head and kissed him softly. 'You're forgiven,' she said gently.

He sighed and she felt him relax. 'Those men you danced with . . .'

Because the words seemed torn from him, she told him quickly, 'They meant nothing.'

He smiled with unmistakable relief and after dropping a swift kiss on her lips released her to start the car. 'I felt like punching their faces in!'

'That shouldn't make me feel better, but it does,' she giggled, thinking of one or two elegant noses that wouldn't have benefited from such treatment.

Slade slanted her a wry glance. 'We always shared the same sense of humour, however twisted.'

Lee suddenly became aware, as he left the drive, that he had turned in the direction of Reading. 'Why aren't you taking me home?' she asked, since it was well after midnight.

'I can't part with you yet.' His mouth tightened. 'And I'm not sharing you with a horde of lodgers who are going to wonder what's going on should we linger too long in the lounge or I followed you upstairs.'

She didn't know why she should feel so reluctant to go with him when they had been apart for three weeks and he was so eager for her company. Yet if he intended proposing, why did he feel it necessary to take her to Reading? Wouldn't his house or hers have been much more appropriate? Whereabouts in Reading could they go to, anyway?

When she asked and was told his flat, she felt more doubtful than ever. 'I'd rather go straight back to River Bend, Slade. The horde of lodgers you refer to are my friends, and they would never intrude.'

'All the same,' he replied with renewed confidence, 'I prefer the flat, and I promise to get you home before daybreak.'

She had forgotten about the flat. It was part of the factory complex but with a separate entrance. 'It's more convenient,' Slade explained as he drew up outside. 'It means I can come and go when I have to be here, without bothering Security.'

No other houses were near and there was no one around, but Lee was still reluctant to go in. Belief that Slade would ask her to marry him was fast fading, and though she hadn't been able to resist him before, this new move of his seemed to reduce what was between them to something oddly distasteful. She had been determined, for her own peace of mind, not to continue allowing herself to be used merely to satisfy his needs, and if she went into the flat with him wouldn't that give exactly the opposite impression? Wouldn't he then be justified in thinking he had every right to make further demands on her?

'I'd still rather go home,' she said stiffly.

'Lee, come here!' he begged, his hands reaching out for her, going expertly over her, drawing her against him fiercely. 'Stop being awkward!'

She winced and drew back, intent on pushing him away, but her resistance didn't even last that long as powerful emotions began sweeping over her. She knew Slade was affected, too, as the eyes fixed on her started smouldering. His breathing changed, becoming short and laboured, while his heart thundered against her as if threatening to leap out of his body. Awed, as always, that she could excite him like this, she forgot everything but the wild warm madness that began pounding through her veins.

Blindly she raised her face and began kissing him, pressing her mouth over the hard bones of his face, giving in to an urgent desire to touch and taste every part of him.

As if her lips tormented beyond endurance, he groaned and his mouth sought hers, his expertise turning it into a sensual experience that left her dizzy and clamouring for more. A deep hunger drove them, increasing the passionate intensity of their embrace until Lee's treacherous body and even her mind was entirely submissive again.

Eventually they had to draw apart in order to breathe. 'Slade,' Lee whispered huskily, feeling his hot breath fanning her face, 'if only this could last for ever!'

He bent his lips to the rapid pulse in her throat and she was shaken by fresh waves of pleasure. 'You're the only woman I want, Lee,' he groaned. 'I haven't brought you here for a one-night stand—you must believe me!'

'If only . . .' she sighed.

He lifted his head with a frown, trying to read her expression in the darkness. 'If only—what?'

'I don't know,' she twisted restlessly. 'Perhaps I wish this wasn't all we had.'

His arms tightened, but his voice was drier. 'I think we have an awful lot that I'm sure neither of us would want to exchange for another kind of relationship for which, as I've already told you, neither of us is suited and which we would soon regret.'

She winced that he sounded so convinced. 'Why should we regret anything that could only make what we already have more secure?'

'Security can kill other things,' he retorted curtly.

'Not if we truly belonged to each other,' she countered, conscious of the pleading note in her voice.

His mouth went stubborn and suddenly he was out of the car, hauling her with him, keeping a tight hold of her while he opened the lift and thrust her into it. 'We have to talk,' he muttered, banging the grille behind them as Lee was still trying to gather her scattered wits. 'I've been making plans while I've been away.'

'Plans?' she queried uncertainly, not sure that she wanted to hear them as the lift shot upwards.

'In a moment,' he said, as they were deposited in a small hall and he operated the complicated combination lock on the floor of the flat. Seconds later he was closing the door behind them and guiding Lee into a spacious lounge. Relieving her of her coat, he threw it over a chair with his own. 'You've never been here before, have you?' he smiled.

'You know I haven't.' She glanced tensely around the comfortable modern room. Her surroundings didn't interest her nearly as much as Slade's face. All his habitual self-assurance had returned. He was smiling, but she only felt depressed. 'What plans have you made?' she asked dully, refusing a drink.

He shrugged and waved her to sit down. When she did he came and sat beside her. 'I want to see more of you,' he said firmly. 'I've been deciding the best way we can live together.'

Lee sighed. It was going to be a repetition of their former argument. 'I've outgrown a no-commitment kind of relationship, Slade,' she retorted, with a kind of impotent weariness.

Impatiently he shot back, 'What else can you suggest for us? We want each other, but otherwise we have little in common. You have to accept that and stop acting childishly.'

Lifting her chin, she asked courageously, 'Is it childish to want something like marriage?'

She could see how her frankness shook him, because he moved restlessly. 'Not for some people, perhaps, but for us it could be a disaster. Besides, it's much easier to part if one hasn't to go through the fuss of a divorce.'

Hurt tore through her. 'I'd still rather marry, Slade.'

She felt his withdrawal even though he slipped a persuasive arm around her. 'We're neither of us the marrying kind, Lee, you know that. I've never pretended to be. I hate being tied and, as we're apparently speaking frankly, I don't believe you have the qualities that make a good wife. You're far too reckless and irresponsible.'

Lee felt her hands perspiring and gripped them tightly. He kept telling her this. Was he trying to convince her or himself? He was offering her an affair, but that wasn't what she wanted. She had sunk her pride by revealing that she would be willing to marry him, but he was only considering his desires, not hers. If he had cared for her, wouldn't hers have had at least some importance?

'Let's do things my way,' he smiled, believing she was weakening towards him.

'It isn't enough,' she replied unsteadily. He didn't begin to understand how she felt, she could see that. If there was nothing standing in their way she believed a man or woman who felt deeply enough to live with each other should be willing, eventually, to make the final commitment. But, she thought bitterly, what happiness would marriage hold for her if Slade didn't love her and was totally against it? If she was unhappy now, how much worse would she feel with a reluctant husband?

'It would be enough,' his eager voice broke through her silent agonising, 'I'd see you had everything you could possibly want.'

'Except you . . .'

He frowned. 'You would have me most of the time, my sweet, but if I had to be away and for some reason couldn't take you with me, you have your writing. I know you're doing extremely well, and I certainly wouldn't be selfish enough to ask you to give it up.'

He kissed her gently, leaving her with the impression that he had decided tender reasoning would get him what he wanted as fast as anything. Restively she struggled from his embrace, feeling too suffocated by his persuasive tones to be able to think clearly. It would be so easy to give in to him, to let him take the burden of everything that worried her off her shoulders. Just to have someone to lean on, to share her troubles as well as her happiness, was a great temptation. But once she began being that dependent on him, how would she ever be able to manage without him when she had to again? And she had told him she had changed. If she gave in to him he might never believe it.

Hot tears spilled down her cheeks and her heart was heavy with confusion. She wanted to be with him always. She loved him, but he considered her as an attractive plaything rather than a partner for life. Yet if she lived with him wouldn't it be better than nothing? No one could fault his generosity, and they were compatible in so many ways. If she had lived with him once, why couldn't she do so again?

But he didn't love her and, after all this time, she feared he never would. And without his love would she ever be happy? She wanted a real marriage, not the pretence of one. Now that she was older, she wanted a future built not only on passion but mutual love and respect.

When Slade had first come back, she had sensed that he was consumed by a savage anger, but tonight this seemed to have been replaced by a much softer emotion. Foolishly, for a while, she had hoped that his feelings for her were deepening into something real and lasting, but she knew that was impossible. He thought no more of her than any other woman he had taken out. She had to say no to him, unless she wanted to see her life in far greater ruins in the years to come than it was today.

'You don't know what you're asking,' she said sharply, realising she had to be strong and drive him away. 'I'd be a fool to let history repeat itself and put myself at your mercy again. I've suddenly discovered I could never be happy with a man like you.'

Her answer visibly shocked him. He had been counting on her capitulation, on her femininity being unable to resist the life of material comfort and sexual bliss he offered. 'A man like me?' he exploded, dark colour washing into his face.

'Slade . . .!'

'You don't have to spell it out,' he snapped. 'I may be a bit slow on the uptake, but I know exactly what you mean. I'm the biggest heel imaginable because I won't fall in with the plans you've made.'

'Plans?' she exclaimed. 'What plans? You were the one making plans. Until just recently I was engaged to your cousin.'

'And then I came back,' green eyes narrowed to a scornful black. 'I thought Matt was the only fool in the family but I needn't have forced you to break your engagement, need I? As soon as you saw I was still attracted, you set your sights higher and would have broken your engagement, anyway. But now you've discovered I'm not as gullible as Matt, you're mad!'

Lee went white and her voice was full of pain. 'Your opinion of me alone should tell you that there's little point in our seeing each other again.'

'You intend returning to Matt or taking up with some other man?'

'No!' Her throat was so tight she could scarcely speak. She had to escape before the hurt he was inflicting tore her to pieces. Jumping up, she made for the door, only to find it firmly locked and Slade right behind her. 'I'm going home!' she cried.

'You aren't going anywhere!' he muttered hoarsely, swinging her about, as pale as she was and just as determined. 'I don't believe you want to. You wouldn't have come with me in the first place unless you'd wanted to.' Savagely his arms tightened, his mouth crushing the hot words she was about to utter back down her throat.

'This is our best line of communication,' he muttered thickly, minutes later against her bruised lips. 'We only argue when we talk.'

Lee was shattered by the burning excitement he aroused and the feverish brilliance of his eyes. By contrast her heart seemed consumed by live pain. 'Take

me home,' she entreated brokenly. 'Let me out and I'll
walk.'

Slade merely laughed, and her teeth chattered as his
hands travelled softly down her body. She couldn't stop
shaking and heard his name on her lips seconds before
he was kissing her senseless again. She struggled,
fighting the surge of desire that went through her as the
heat of it threatened to melt her resistance. It frightened
her that Slade was able to demolish it so easily.

'Don't!' she succeeded in getting the strangled gasp
past his marauding lips.

He took no notice. He was using force to subdue her,
until the hunger he knew he could arouse in her grew
too overwhelming for her to do anything about it. His
amusement and disregard for her wishes gave her the
strength to continue struggling, but all she achieved was
her own exhaustion.

'Lee, be sensible,' he groaned, his voice thick but with
a tenseness about it that suggested he was fighting for
more than just immediate victory.

'I am being sensible,' she gasped, like a drowning
swimmer being swept out to sea. 'You're the one who's
not!'

He went on kissing her, parting her trembling lips,
delving deep. When at last she began clinging to him,
ardently returning his kisses, he asked with a hint of
hardness in his voice, 'Can you honestly insist now that
you don't want me?'

Completely lost, Lee was incapable of answering. Her
heart was beating so loudly she didn't hear the
weakening voice of reason. She merely gazed at him
blindly, her blue eyes fixed helplessly on his hard,
sensual mouth. As it moved triumphantly towards her
own, her eyes closed, her arms going round his neck, a
betraying sigh of pleasure on her lips.

His kisses had a new urgency, a flaring hunger that
she knew she felt herself. She lay against him, weakly
yielding, her hands stroking his thick dark hair, making

no further protest when he lifted her and carried her across the lounge to one of the bedrooms and laid her on a wide,.soft bed.

- Her dress tore as he slid down her zip and removed it with something less than his usual skill. He lay beside her, pressing his lips to the creamy skin of her throat, and as his mouth travelled lower she felt the growing urgency inside both of them. A dizzying weakness flooded her as his passionate lovemaking extinguished the last remnants of her will to fight him. When his mouth found her breasts, he was breathing hard, murmuring something she didn't even hear, and she was writhing with pleasure, her eyes closed tight.

Vaguely she was aware of an odd tenderness entering his voice as he pushed her back among the pillows, but nothing was able to penetrate the trance of her growing desire. His black head moved against her body, his hands and mouth warm on her naked skin, and she was trapped by an incredible excitement that had her shaking. His fiercely muttered words of remorse and love merely blended indistinctly with the deafening noise her heart was making.

Hazily she saw his broad shoulders, his hard-muscled chest coming nearer, and she wrapped her arms around his back, caressing him as she melted into him. Their bodies pressed closer and joined in a rhythmic movement that intensified as their passion flared out of control.

There was a new violence about Slade in that moment, but she was helpless to meet it with anything other than complete response. She arched against him, an inability to breathe torturing her as she was swept into a union more devastating than anything she had known before. He seemed intent on stamping an indelible brand on her. Without mercy he imposed himself on her, until the blinding surges of ecstasy he was arousing brought a shattering release. Eyes closed, Lee lay quivering, her arms still clasped around his neck, but with a feeling of coldness returning to rapidly steal the warmth from her body as reality returned with it.

As he lay slumped against her in an attitude that in another man she might have taken for defeat, she took her arms away and tried to escape, but he wouldn't let her. As she slid from under him, his hand jerked out to hold her. Raising on an elbow, he stared with hot eyes at her perfectly formed body. Through her gathering tears, she saw his jaw clench as he read the depth of her regret. 'You hate me, don't you?'

Hate? She was near to believing it. Slade gave her so much pleasure, but, in bitter retrospect, this was something she could only feel ashamed of. She felt suddenly degraded, and it must have showed, for his face went white.

'Don't you?' he insisted harshly.

'Right now, yes.'

'Damn you!' he said hoarsely. 'You'd better get dressed.'

Lee nodded dully. There was something final in his voice that she should have welcomed, but it seemed to hit her like a blow and she couldn't help but feel that something between them had ended. He turned, sliding abruptly off the other side of the bed, but not before she had seen a new hardness enter his face. Wonderingly her eyes followed his tall naked figure as he picked up his clothes and left the room abruptly. She swallowed hard and felt the new deadly coldness sweeping over her again.

Slade was waiting for her in the lounge, and she was struck afresh by the grimness of his expression. His eyes, dark and blank, rested on her soberly while she waited for him to speak.

As she stood before him, pale-faced and trembling, he swallowed, as though a constriction in his throat hurt him. 'You don't have to be frightened of me anymore, Lee,' he said, with such unmistakable self-contempt that she flinched.

Because she could have sworn this was the first time in his life he had ever felt ashamed of himself, she felt confused. She wanted to talk to him, but though she spoke his name, she could find nothing more in the vast emptiness that seemed to be her mind. The depression settling on her so heavily allowed no constructive thought to get through.

For a moment she could only stare at him, conscious of a despairing love for him. He had dressed, but seemed indifferent that his hair was still tousled. There was an air about him that suggested he had been making decisions which he hadn't found easy. He seemed tense and unrelaxed, his mouth grim.

Suddenly Lee wanted to go to him and offer what comfort she could, but he offered no encouragement, and her nerve failed. He didn't care for her, he had never cared for her! Every time they met there was a flare-up of sexual attraction, and tonight she had rashly goaded him and he had lost control. He had used the full and dangerous force of his powerful sexuality in an attempt to subdue her to his way of thinking, but somehow this had worked against him. Now he felt ashamed of himself and, with his usual arrogance, didn't relish the emotion. Now he only wanted to be rid of her, so he shouldn't be constantly reminded of it.

Wrenching her eyes from his, she stumbled past him to find her coat, but, defining her intentions, Slade beat her to it. Automatically the gentleman, she thought cynically, as he draped it around her shoulders, then jumped as his hand touched her arm and an electric shock shot through her.

'I only intend taking you home,' he said icily, mistaking her reaction.

She gulped, and as his eyes noted the suffering etched on her beautiful features, his face darkened as he clearly judged that she was terrified of him. A mixture of pain and fury was expressed in his voice as he rasped, 'Haven't I told you, you have nothing to fear from me any more, Lee.'

'I know,' she whispered numbly.

'I didn't think it mattered to me how you felt, but it does . . .'

'Slade?'

'You don't have to keep repeating how much you hate me,' he muttered. 'I'm believing it at last. I find I'm not even sure that I'm interested in the kind of life I had mapped out for us five minutes ago. You say you've changed in the past five years, and maybe so have I.'

She was suddenly angry at the undisguised contempt he displayed, not guessing that it was directed entirely against himself. 'If we're both disillusioned it must be your fault!' she cried, her red hair bouncing about her flushed face, giving a magnificent wildness to her temper. 'You always take what you want, don't you? You never stop to consider how your victims feel. If you're finally catching on that sex isn't enough, I doubt if it will have any lasting effect on your insatiable appetites!'

She had gone too far—he went white. There was a stony silence, broken only by Lee's ragged breathing. 'Are you through?' he asked, with such deadly coldness that Lee knew she would never be forgiven. 'You may act like an outraged virgin, but your sexual needs always matched my own. I only took what you were very willing to give. And I paid top rates, remember?'

Lee stared at him, her anger dying fast as his glance roamed insolently over her. There was hunger in his eyes but also a hate which betrayed clearly that if he ever touched her again it would only be in revenge. Summoning the tattered remains of her pride, she lifted her chin. 'You talk as though I demanded payment for everything!'

'But your last demand I refuse to meet.'

'You mean your freedom,' she scorned. 'You wouldn't part with that for anything.'

He winced but replied curtly, 'No woman has taken it from me yet, nor ever will.'

For Lee that was the end of everything. There was nothing more to say. 'I hate you!' she breathed, not because Slade had asked her not to repeat it, but because it seemed the only retort suitable for a remark that spelt the end of her dreams.

He went rigid. 'If it's any comfort to you,' he said stiffly, 'I hate myself for a lot of things. Now can we leave?'

As he slammed into the car with her, the biting words he seemed about to utter died as he saw the tears streaming down her cheeks. Producing a clean handkerchief, he dropped it in her lap, then turned away. As she picked it up, Lee saw a muscle working in his throat and noticed his hands clenched on the steering wheel. She had a feeling that if she sank her pride and appealed to him, she could soon be in his arms again. But she wanted no false sympathy, or sympathy of any kind, for that matter. If she couldn't have his love, she wanted nothing else, for anything else would merely serve to prolong her ultimate agony.

Later, when Slade dropped her at River Bend, she managed to thank him and say goodbye with a cool little smile which she hoped denied her former tears and concealed her heartache. For his part, Slade merely nodded grimly and drove off, leaving her standing staring after him until his lights disappeared and the drive and her life was in darkness again.

The next morning, Julia teased, 'You were the belle of the ball—and the talk of it, Lee.'

'And a dark horse!' quipped Sandra. 'You never told us you were so thick with the most eligible man around. One of the most,' she amended, obviously thinking of Matt.

Lee was glad it was her turn to cook breakfast, but

she tried to hide a white face, not blushes. 'If you're referring to Slade Western, I don't suppose I'll be seeing him again.' With her attention focussed on the eggs she was frying, she managed to retain a light note. 'Naïve country girls aren't really much in his line.'

'That wasn't the impression everyone got last night,' Sandra persisted.

'Well, he didn't ask to see me again,' Lee retorted, and was glad she had stuck to the truth when he made no attempt to during the following weeks.

After several days had gone by and he didn't try and get in touch with her, she realised he had accepted her decision and wasn't going to. Although Lee was still sure she had made the right decision, she hadn't guessed how dreadful it would make her feel. There were times when Nigel spoke of him, when she felt like dropping everything to go and find him, to beg to be allowed to live with him under any conditions he chose.

When she had fled from Slade in Paris, she had been heartbroken, but the subsequent loss of her memory had cushioned her from the worst effects of this. Yet, without her being aware of it, in the period between that date and now, her love for him had apparently deepened, making the pain she had known then seem like a mere ache compared with what she was presently suffering. She saw clearly that her involvement with Matt had been a terrible mistake. At least, Slade in his ruthlessness had saved her from a marriage that could only have ended in disaster. Perhaps one day she might be able to put Slade from her mind and love again, but it would be criminal to even think of another man until she had managed to get rid of Slade's image completely.

Julia and Sandra quickly tired of teasing her, Slade's failure to appear at River Bend convincing them eventually that Slade's interest in Lee had indeed only been transitory. Only Matt now looked at her curiously, as she grew paler and thinner, something the others didn't seem to notice, but she avoided the concern she saw in his eyes, the questions hovering on his lips she had no wish to answer. She breathed a sigh of relief that Sandra kept him well occupied, though their absorption in each other seemed in a way to only emphasise her own loneliness. She was pleased, for Matt's sake, that he had found someone else and realised that soon she might be in danger of losing all her lodgers.

Though she knew Slade was still at Reading, she was so seldom in the town herself that she never expected to bump into him. It was exactly three weeks after the night of the barbecue that she did. Having spent long hours on her last book, rather than brood continually over him, she had finished it very quickly and was trying to decide whether to post it to her publisher or deliver it herself, when Dulcie rang to ask if she would have Trigg for a couple of days.

Lee agreed happily, glad of anything, now that she had finished her book, that might provide further distraction. She could shelve the decision about posting it until after Trigg had gone. The first afternoon she drove him in to Reading to find him a manual on model railways which he wanted, and it was in the bookshop that she bumped into Mrs Western and Slade.

Trigg saw them first and announced in far too loud a voice, 'Lee, there's the man who stole your bike with the lady who took us on the river! Do you think he's going to steal her boat?'

Lee hushed Trigg as several amused heads turned, but she couldn't prevent her cheeks heating. She couldn't be sure that Slade had heard, for he continued his appraisal of a row of paperbacks, but his mother did and immediately came over. 'Hello, young man,' she laughed at Trigg, 'you do make the most frightful accusations!' And to Lee, 'How lovely to see you, dear. The last time we met in Reading, it was here. How are you keeping?'

'F-fine,' Lee faltered brightly. 'And you?'

When Mrs Western said she was very well, Lee hurried on, averting her eyes from Slade's firmly turned back, 'Trigg and I are looking for a book on trains.'

'I'm staying with Lee again,' Trigg smiled at Lee lovingly, 'while my parents are in London.'

While Mrs Western asked Trigg the precise name of the book he was after, Lee stole another glance at Slade. She got a shock to discover he was now standing only a few feet away, regarding her bitterly. He looked as grim and as distant as when she had last seen him and, like herself, thinner. His face was set with a stiff, cold expression that sent a shiver right through her. But as their eyes met she saw nothing in them to give even the slightest clue to his feelings. She might have been a stranger; they were entirely blank.

# CHAPTER NINE

LEE took several deep breaths as, despite Slade's coldness, desire for him flamed into life. The dark force of his eyes seemed to weld with hers and as his gaze narrowed she felt as though she had been hit by something hard. She heard Mrs Western asking if she had finished her latest book and nodded without being really aware of what she was doing.

She felt suddenly ill. Mrs Western's question, though, did succeed in distracting her numbed attention away from Slade. 'I'm taking or sending it to London, next week.'

'I'm sure your publisher will like it.' Lydia's eyes were warm with approval. 'You must come to dinner, one evening, Thursday perhaps, and you can tell me about it. Would Thursday suit you, Slade?'

Lee followed Lydia's questioning glance uncertainly. He wouldn't want her dining with his mother. It didn't take any great astuteness to read his thoughts. Did he really believe she wanted to accept, knowing that being in his home would only remind her of the last evening she had spent there? He wouldn't be there if he knew she was coming, but would that make her feel any better?

'I'd love to,' she replied, forcing a pleased smile. She had been about to refuse, but Slade's indifferent shrug had taken so much of the eagerness from Lydia's face that she couldn't bring herself to risk removing it altogether.

'That will be wonderful!' beamed Lydia, quickly diverted. 'Slade seldom brings a pretty girl to see me, nowadays. In fact, I can't remember the last time. It must be years . . .'

Slade interrupted shortly, 'I'm sure Miss Moreau isn't interested in what I do in my spare time.'

'Miss Moreau?' His mother's eyes widened innocently, 'How stiff you sound, Slade, but you remind me that Lee is half French. Do you keep in touch with your French relations, Lee?'

'No,' Lee hesitated. 'I'm thinking of looking them up, though, before I begin my next book. I could spend several weeks in France.'

Slade's brows grew blacker, but he made no comment.

'That would make a pleasant change,' exclaimed Lydia. 'And you never know—you might even meet someone special and decide to settle there. The French are very attractive,' she teased. 'I could come and stay with you for your first christening.'

'Lee must be quite capable of planning her own life,' snapped Slade, a peculiar white line around his mouth.

'But she looks as if she could do with a holiday,' his mother frowned. 'How much weight have you lost since I last saw you, child?'

'A lot, my mother says,' piped Trigg.

'I've been slimming,' Lee hedged, then invented an excuse to hurry Trigg away. She smiled weakly at Lydia, a smile which somehow slid to include Slade, but he merely stared at her grimly, his hard face as forbidding as ever.

Lee was so shaken by the encounter that it took her a while to get over it. If she could have got out of her promise to dine with Mrs Western she would have done, but when Lydia rang to confirm the arrangement, her nerve failed her. Although Slade wouldn't be there, she would be going to his home and, with every bit of her so sensitively attuned to him, she was sure she would feel his presence everywhere. It took a great deal of courage not to say no.

As Mrs Western always dressed for dinner, Lee chose a simple black dress that seemed to match her mood yet looked well with her gleaming red hair. By making up carefully, she managed to conceal the dark shadows under her eyes and a little blusher disguised the paleness of her cheeks. She put on a pair of flat shoes for driving and took some high-heeled black sandals to change into when she arrived.

To her consternation, Slade was there. He didn't let her in, there was a butler to do that, but he was in the lounge pouring drinks. Lee almost turned and ran when she caught sight of him, resplendent in full evening dress, his international playboy image well to the fore. During the course of the evening, Lee was to come to suspect that he had dressed magnificently on purpose to show her what she had given up, but in that moment his assured masculinity so took her breath away that she was unable to think of anything, except, perhaps, the rate her heart was beating.

He regarded her silently, making no move to welcome her, and when she recovered sufficient poise to look around, she saw to her surprise that there were several other guests. Mrs Western, when Lee forced her numb legs in her direction, murmured apologetically that Slade had invited some friends at the last minute, leaving Lee with no alternative but to smile and murmur, 'How nice!'

Slade continued to stare at her so coldly that she feared it would be noticed. When he thrust a glass in her hands containing a drink she didn't immediately recognise, she wondered if it was poison. Certainly he looked just about as friendly. The other guests consisted of three couples whom she hadn't seen before. Before dinner had progressed very far, she discovered they were actually business associates, and she wondered why Slade had arranged for them to be here on this particular evening. It didn't take long before she thought she understood. These people weren't close friends, so the conversation had to be general. He had been determined to be here, himself, to see that Lee didn't corrupt Lydia or steal from her in any way, but he had resolved that it shouldn't be an intimate occasion.

The only time a more personal note crept in was when one of the strangers mentioned touring in France, and Lydia, obviously becoming aware that Slade was excluding Lee as far as possible from the conversation, said quickly, 'Miss Moreau has relations in—the Dordogne, isn't it, Lee?'

'Yes,' Lee smiled at the couple concerned. 'I haven't met them yet, but I did get as far as that a few years ago. Unfortunately I met with an accident.'

'Were you badly injured?' the woman asked with a sympathetic glance. 'Traffic over there goes so fast!'

Wishing she had never mentioned it, with Slade's glance suddenly rapier-sharp, Lee moved her head negatively and muttered something about losing her memory.

'She's going back again,' Lydia jumped to her rescue. 'The next time we dine together, perhaps you'll be able to compare notes? Lee's father was French, but her mother was Belinda Farrell, the actress, you know.'

Lee was the focus of attention now, she suspected much to Slade's chagrin. 'Oh, how marvellous!' a middle-aged blonde lady cried. 'I was a great fan of Miss Farrell's. I thought her last film, *The Night the Rains Came*, was wonderful. Of course she was very popular.'

Someone else said, 'You resemble her, Miss Moreau, but I presume you don't act?'

After a few more such queries, which Lee answered as best as she could, Slade changed the subject firmly. Lee sensed that he was angry with his mother for introducing it and impatient of the questions his guests were asking, but she refused to believe he was acting protectively.

An hour later, when he was called to his study to take a call from the States, she decided to go home. She was disturbed by the way his eyes had seldom left her all evening and felt she could stay no longer. If he had looked at her kindly, she might have borne it, but the icy condemnation in his eyes left her cold and shivering. While he was otherwise engaged, she took the opportunity to escape.

Lydia didn't want her to leave as early, but Lee had made up her mind. Quickly she kissed Lydia good night and said she would be in touch. Yet as she drove away, she couldn't help gazing through the rear mirror of her car at Slade's home and wondering what the future could hold for her without him.

The next afternoon she called at The Willows with a pair of socks that Trigg had left behind. Dulcie didn't always make her welcome, but for once she seemed genuinely pleased to see her.

'Thank goodness for someone to talk to!' she cried, dragging Lee inside when she would as soon have gone straight home. 'I had a terrible argument with George last night over Trigg—I just have to tell someone or burst!'

Thinking it more than likely that Dulcie had already discussed it with half the neighbourhood, Lee allowed herself to be pushed into a chair and tried to look attentive. Trigg's parents were always quarrelling about him, she doubted if they'd ever agreed on anything concerning him since the day he was born. When Dulcie mentioned boarding school, however, Lee's ears pricked apprehensively. So it was that again!

'We got some papers to sign,' Dulcie explained. 'I arranged everything, it's not as if George has had to bother, but instead of being grateful he thinks we should wait. Until I actually did something about it he was quite agreeable, but now he just refuses to see my point of view and I don't think he ever will.'

Lee concealed a wry smile. George, like many men, chose the line of least resistance until cornered. 'Why don't you wait another year or two, as I've already suggested?' she advised discreetly. 'Then both George and Trigg might feel differently.'

Dulcie jumped up and paced the room in agitation. 'Why can't you agree with me sometimes?'

'I'm not taking sides,' Lee said patiently. 'I'm simply giving my opinion. But I do think a lot of Trigg—and you,' she added hastily.

'Beats me why!' Dulcie retorted sharply, but Lee could see she was partly mollified. 'Ah, well,' she sighed, 'you might as well stay for a cuppa, now you're here. It won't take a second.'

'And Trigg?' Lee asked tentatively, a little uneasy that Dulcie had changed the subject so quickly. He would be miserable at boarding school and she couldn't help feeling concerned.

'I suppose I may as well forget it,' Dulcie sighed, then confessed rather sheepishly, 'I guess I'd really made up my mind before you arrived, but it's not easy to admit you're wrong and everyone else is right.'

Lee left soon afterwards. She didn't feel so good, and Dulcie's lukewarm tea hadn't helped. It didn't make her feel any better, either, to find Slade in the drive when she got home. She knew her face was pale as she parked her car and walked towards him. What on earth did he want? She would have walked straight past him if he hadn't spoken.

'Lee!' Savagely he leapt from the gleaming monster he drove and caught up with her. 'I've been waiting hours!'

'Have you?' she answered distantly. He was biting words off in a way that made her feel distinctly nervous, but she tried to appear cool. Her heart seemed to be in her throat and a dizzying sensation was making her head spin. Again she wondered why he was here.

He followed her inside without waiting for the invitation she didn't proffer. Lee stumbled into the kitchen, not turning until she reached the table. For a burning moment, as their eyes met she almost wilted under the sheer intensity of his gaze.

'This isn't a social call,' he muttered thickly.

She tried to resist an overwhelming desire to throw her arms around him, to confess how terrible the past weeks had been without him, but of course that was impossible. His attitude towards her hadn't changed, and she had her pride.

'What do you want?' she breathed.

'An explanation,' he replied curtly.

She realised he was furious over something—but what? 'Would you mind explaining?' she asked carefully.

'The explaining's for you to do,' he retorted sharply. 'I want to know exactly what happened in France after you left me!'

Lee gasped as she recalled the remark she had made at dinner, the previous evening. All her life she had been too impulsive, you'd think at twenty-five she would have learned! Her remark must have seemed to Slade like a challenge he had to get to the bottom of. Yet what right had he to demand anything, when everything was over between them?

'It's none of your business,' she muttered stubbornly. 'Anyway, why should I satisfy your idle curiosity?'

'Idle curiosity!' he cursed under his breath. 'My God, Lee! Haven't you any idea what I went through in Paris after you left? I was desperate to find you.'

'You were?' A dazed kind of glow entered Lee's eyes.

Suddenly he seemed aware of what he was saying and a cooler expression replaced the heat in his face. 'You were nineteen. Wouldn't that alone be a good enough reason to worry over you? I was thirty, remember.'

So he had only been worried. 'You could have checked with Grandfather,' she said dully.

Slade grasped her shoulders, his eyes murderous. 'I had already checked, without his knowledge, and saw no point in alarming him unduly.'

'Your hired spies, I suppose?'

'Don't look so scornful, Lee,' he snapped. 'They're sometimes necessary.'

'So you decided I'd gone off with another man?'

'Until,' his eyes darkened, 'we were together again.'

She felt her heart thud violently as he stared at her, unreadable expressions chasing over his face. His throat moved, as if something had just rocked his deepest emotions. Was he remembering the tempestuous passion of their reunion, her confession that he was the only man she had ever known? A film of sweat broke out on his brow and she stared at it curiously.

'Slade?'

Ignoring the enquiring note in her voice, he rasped, 'So what was all that about losing your memory?'

She sighed, feeling unequal to further defiance. 'I told you, I was trying to find my French relations. My mother always said she didn't like them, but I don't think she ever knew them, and after I left you I decided to look them up. I still owed you eighteen months and I thought if they took me in I would be safe.'

He winced, his mouth tightening, as if he'd been hit somewhere where it hurt. 'And . . .?'

'I'm not sure,' she confessed. 'I was hitch-hiking and it got dark. I only recall seeing some lights coming up behind me, then everything went black. The driver of whatever it was that hit me couldn't have seen me, because he didn't stop. I was found wandering by some people the next morning and they took me to the nuns in a nearby convent. I wasn't badly injured and they—the nuns, that is—looked after me until my memory returned. That's all.'

'All!' His face darkened with the savage force of his emotions. 'You might have been killed!'

'I'm sorry,' she said helplessly. 'I suppose I was young and foolish and didn't stop to think. After my memory returned I came back, and Grandfather was ill.'

Slade drew a deep breath, as if trying to put some devastating picture behind him. Lee frowned as she noticed how pale he had gone. If she had been killed, did he believe he might have got the blame? For several minutes he didn't speak, then he said slowly, 'Matt mentioned that you'd nursed your grandfather?'

'Julia and I together.'

'Over a year.'

Lee coloured faintly. 'It was the least I could do, after neglecting him for a year.' She raised eyes so clearly blue that there was no doubting her sincerity. 'I did nothing out of a sense of duty. I think Grandfather knew that and died content.'

Slade was silent again, studying her with a mixed expression. 'Nursing an old man must have been quite a change for you?'

She took the odd note in his voice for dryness and flinched. 'Six months in a convent hospital taught me a lot. The nuns were kind but strict. I learned a lot of things about nursing and caring for the sick. I also learned to recognise the difference between true values and false ones. I told you I'd changed.'

'Not physically.'

Her delicate features paled. 'Is that the only way you ever see me, Slade?'

'No,' he denied curtly, clenching his hands. 'Lee,' he went on tautly, 'I've got something to ask you, but what time will your friends be back?'

'They shouldn't be long.'

While she was wondering why that seemed important, he appeared to reach a decision. 'When are you going to London? From what you were saying to Lydia, I gathered it's to be soon.'

Where was the connection between the question he wanted to ask and her trip to London? 'Monday.'

'How do you intend travelling?'

'By car,' she frowned.

'I'll take you,' he said firmly. 'I'll pick you up early. What I have in mind, I hope, will take the whole morning.'

This frightened Lee somehow. 'I'd as soon drive myself.'

He stared at her closely. 'You don't look fit enough.'

'I'll be all right,' she protested. 'I caught a slight chill a week or two ago and it seems to have gone to my stomach. I'll get something at the chemist's tomorrow.'

'You're far too thin as well,' he observed grimly, 'so don't argue. And I have to go to town on Monday, anyway. I have an appointment in the afternoon which I can't miss, so I'll pick you up about nine——'

To Lee's stunned surprise he bent and kissed her as he said goodbye, but his departure was so swift that she had no chance to enquire what it was all about. He might have kissed her for many reasons—impulse being the most probable. Certainly, as he had left, his face had been too hard and strained to allow her to imagine anything between them had changed. Perhaps it was for Lydia's sake that he had decided to be more friendly. Maybe he thought that a pretence of friendship might arouse his mother's antagonism less than outright enmity. Lee sighed as she began preparing dinner. Friendship from a man was cold comfort when she wanted his love.

When the casserole she was preparing was safely in the oven, she rang Mrs Western to thank her for what she had to pretend had been a lovely evening, and Lydia was inclined to chat.

'It's so nice having someone to talk to. Slade's been busy all day. He's having important discussions with some Middle East delegates about electronics and I don't expect to see much of him all weekend. Then on Monday, I believe he has another meeting with one of them in London. I was telling him he works far too hard. Like you, he's getting far too thin.'

It seemed the unanimous verdict, Lee thought wryly, as Lydia rang off, but how could she eat when her appetite was non-existent and even the sight of food made her feel sick? She blamed the cold she'd had, but she didn't know about Slade. He had always worked too hard; his mother was probably right.

The weekend passed slowly. Julia and Nigel went off until the Tuesday evening to visit Julia's parents, while Sandra had arranged to stay with Matt's parents for a few days to give his mother another break as his father was ill again. Lee wasn't lonely, but the house seemed empty, as it always did when she was by herself in it. She could have gone out or had some friends in, but she couldn't find the necessary energy. On Sunday she decided she would spend at least one night in London. There was shopping she could do. It would be fun. She tried to whip up enthusiasm. She might even have her hair done.

She was still not sure what to make of Slade's offer to take her, but she wasn't looking forward to it. They wouldn't be good company for each other and she wished he hadn't suggested it.

On Sunday, before she went to bed, she set her alarm for seven the next morning, intending to be up and away before he arrived. She didn't trust herself not to make a fool of herself if she had to spend even an hour alone with him, and felt she would rather suffer his anger than her own inevitable humiliation.

But as soon as she got out of bed on Monday, she knew she wouldn't be going anywhere; she felt too ill. She sat still, hoping she was mistaken, but whenever she tried to move her stomach heaved. Her head ached as well and she couldn't stop trembling. Unhappily she crawled back under the sheets, thinking if she stayed there for a while she might be able to get downstairs and make a cup of tea.

The tablets she had got from the chemist couldn't have worked, though she had felt better yesterday. Weakly she watched the curtains wafting on the breeze coming in through the open window. Before she left she must remember to check the windows. Autumn was upon them and there were bound to be a few storms.

The weather looked far from promising, this morning. Nothing looked promising this morning, she thought dully, falling into a fitful doze.

When she woke again, she lay for a minute, then determinedly dragged herself out of bed and downstairs to the kitchen. It was after eight and she still felt terrible. She wished she could contact Slade, to tell him not to call, but where would he be? There was a chance that he might have changed his mind and not turn up.

Deciding to trust he wouldn't, she boiled the kettle and put a coffee bag in a cup. Coffee seemed to help her more than tea, lately. Then she made some toast, but though she was determined to eat it, she found herself still sitting staring at it ten minutes later.

The knock on the door startled her, yet she knew it could only be Slade. Panic struck her, though she had been expecting him, and she went unsteadily to answer it. He was wearing a grey three-piece suit and looked so smart that she felt like a tramp by comparison and wished she could sink through the floor.

'I've decided against going to London,' she muttered, as he frowned. 'Neither of them said good morning.

'What's wrong, Lee?' Slade asked abruptly.

'Nothing,' she bluffed. 'Can't a girl change her mind?'

'Not the way you're doing it,' he snapped, his eyes all over her. 'You look ill.'

She hugged her thin robe about her tightly. 'I—I'm sorry, I slept in. I didn't realise the time, but I'm definitely not going. I'll post my manuscript.'

'Hi, not so fast!' he rasped as she began closing the door. 'Do you really think I could go anywhere with you like this? What the devil's wrong with you, anyway, Lee? You're like a scarecrow and your face hasn't any colour. You used to be able to go practically night and day without any sleep. There has to be some reason for such a change!'

Lee's mouth set sulkily. 'I've still got plenty of energy

most of the time—and I can do without such flattering remarks!'

'You're getting them, all the same,' he snapped, pushing her inside and slamming the door. 'Where were you, or can't you remember?'

'In the kitchen.' She stared at him resentfully through the thick curtain of her red hair and flinched when he grabbed hold of a brush lying on the hall table and with a few quick strokes restored it to order. 'That's better,' he said more gently. 'Now lead on, Delilah.'

She should have protested, but how could she when she could scarcely find the strength to walk? How dared he walk in here and begin ordering her about? Did he think he was making her feel any better? Yet wasn't she glad to see him? She lowered heavy lids to conceal sudden tears as she endeavoured not to give way to the impulse to lean on him in self-pity.

'Is that your breakfast?' he asked, tight-lipped as she sat down.

'Yes.' She hoped he didn't notice the toast was soggy and cold.

He did. Looking at it distastefully, he said, 'That was made long before you answered the door. Why aren't you eating?'

She pushed her coffee aside, which was a mistake because he saw that was cold too. 'I haven't had much appetite lately,' she prevaricated.

'I noticed you ate nothing for dinner on Thursday.'

Well, he would, wouldn't he, as he had never taken his eyes off her. 'I'm sure I did,' she defied woodenly.

'You gave an admirable display on how to push food around a plate,' he retorted, adding, when she merely shrugged, 'You always ate well, especially at breakfast.'

'Gluttonously.'

'I didn't say that.' His jaw set stubbornly. 'My God, Lee, I'm just trying to discover what's the matter with you—not criticising! How would you feel if I looked like death, losing weight and everything? You're far too young to look the way you do and there not to be anything wrong with you? Have you seen a doctor?'

'No.'

'Wouldn't that be a sensible thing to do?'

'I'll get round to it sometime. If,' she qualified quickly, 'this bug I seem to have caught doesn't clear up. One can't always be running to a doctor, wasting his time when others need him more urgently.'

'When did you last see one?' asked Slade sarcastically.

When her grandfather was ill, but she wasn't going to tell him about that. 'Would you like some coffee?' she asked, struggling to her feet and reaching for the kettle.

'Here, let me. You sit down,' he pushed her into her chair when she began to object, 'Lee, for heaven's sake!'

She collapsed in a shivering heap, physically unable to fight him. 'Bully!' she muttered childishly.

'At the moment that might be exactly what you're in need of!'

There was a quality of steel in his voice, a sharpness in his eyes as he regarded her. Lee bit her lip, looking ready to shatter like fragile glass. Weakly she subsided and obediently drank the hot tea he made. Because he seemed anxious, she even tried to eat the fresh toast he produced, in order to placate him.

'Haven't I made it the way you like? Or is it the tea?'

She couldn't have inherited her parent's acting abilities. 'I've gone off tea lately. I've been having coffee.'

'You used to dislike it for breakfast.'

'My tastes must have changed.'

Slade paused, shrugged, then poured himself a cup of tea and sat down opposite, watching her closely. The paleness of her face, as well as her thinness, worried him, but he kept any compassion from his eyes as she might be quick to take advantage of it and ignore her toast. 'Eat up,' he commanded sternly.

There was a strained tenseness in the silence between

them. Each eyed the other suspiciously. Slade's heavy sigh seemed to betray something, but his arrogant kind of patience angered her. Opposing Slade was like challenging a brick wall, you only came away with bruises. If she had learned nothing else, all the years she had known him, she had learned that! She ate her toast slowly, feeling rather like a child who has been wrongly chastised, but was relieved to find his austere treatment working.

'Feeling better?' he asked, when she finished.

'Yes,' she was forced to admit, if not willingly.

'How about London, then? There's still time.'

'No.' She knew she couldn't face it.

His eyes darkened. 'You mean you don't want to go with me?'

Lee shut her eyes, her thoughts splintered. She didn't want to answer his question. She was trying to insulate herself in a dark void with no emotions allowed to enter. She couldn't have gone to London with anyone, this morning, but even if she had felt completely well, she wouldn't have gone with him. Knowing everything between them was over, the pain she endured, whenever she was with him was rapidly becoming more than she could bear.

Swallowing back tears, she jumped up, about to ask him to go, but before she could get anything out she realised she had moved too quickly. Words clogged in her throat as the room tilted and swung in the most alarming fashion.

'Lee!'

Slade caught her as she swayed, his glance glittering apprehensively over her paper-white face. Trembling, he lifted her in his arms and carried her to the comfortable cushioned settle that stood against the kitchen wall.

'I'm all right,' she whispered, wondering where her head was and if her stomach was thinking of leaving her. 'You shouldn't have upset me.'

He laid her gently down. 'Is that what I do?'

'Yes—no ...' Fresh tears washed her eyes as his tender expression and incredibly gentle voice seemed to take any sting from his firmer tones as he went on, 'As for being all right, as you put it, if a piece of dry toast can make you feel ill then you're far from it. You're going to see a doctor.'

'One nearly always has to have an appointment,' she protested, 'unless it's an emergency.'

'This is one.' His mouth tightened inexorably. 'I'm taking you to see my doctor, so don't argue. He happens to be a personal friend of mine.'

Slade didn't even bother to telephone. He arrived at the surgery, demanding immediate attention for Lee and, amazingly, it seemed to her, she was given it. It must have something to do with his friend happening to be free, she thought, otherwise it would surely have been impossible.

Half an hour later, after being assured by the doctor that he couldn't find anything wrong with her but that he would be in touch as soon as the results of one or two tests he was making came through, she waited in the car while Slade spoke to him. When Slade returned, looking far from displeased, she felt relieved. Whatever his friend had said to him had certainly removed much of the former grimness from his expression.

Nevertheless, he still seemed concerned for her and insisted that she rested immediately she got home. He made her sit with her feet up in the lounge and fussed over her so protectively that she knew she had to get rid of him before she decided she couldn't do without all the care and attention he was showering on her. He even cooked her a light lunch and watched over her like a watchdog to see that she ate it, a bemused expression that puzzled her on his face.

Suddenly he glanced sharply at the clock. 'Oh, lord, I nearly forgot!' he exclaimed. 'I have a meeting in London this afternoon that I can't miss. I would,' he frowned, 'if it wasn't for so many people depending on me. Will you be all right until I get back, darling?'

'I should be,' Lee smiled at him gratefully, 'after all you've done for me.'

'I'll be home early,' he promised. 'I still have something to ask you.'

Wondering what it was, she smiled at him, feeling very much in his debt and aware of a new warmth that seemed to be flowing out of him towards her. Perhaps in the future, if they could even be friends, it might go a little way towards relieving some of her heartache.

After he had gone, she went slowly upstairs and after taking a shower, lay on her bed. The light mixture which Slade's doctor had given her must have worked, for now she felt lethargic and pleasantly drowsy, rather than ill. Eventually she slept, and it was after six when she woke.

The telephone was ringing. It must have woken her up. 'Not before time!' she muttered, with a horrified glance at her watch as she answered it.

It could be Slade! Her heart leapt as she rolled over and reached for the extension by her bedside. 'River Bend,' she said breathlessly.

It wasn't Slade, it was Dulcie Mansfield. As Lee's spirits dropped several degrees, Dulcie asked angrily, 'Wherever have you been, Lee? I came round, but your door was locked and I couldn't get an answer. Trigg's disappeared, and I wondered if you knew where he is.'

'No.' Lee swung her feet to the floor and tried to sharpen her sleep-dulled wits. 'I'm sorry, he isn't here and I've no idea where he might be. How long has he been gone?'

'Over three hours.'

'Three hours!' That could mean another two or three, on Dulcie's calculations.

'Lee, please!' Dulcie exclaimed. 'No lectures, not right now. He's nearly nine, and after lunch he said he was going to play in the old shed at the bottom of our garden. George is helping him fix his model railway there as it makes a mess in the house. I was doing a few things and then I realised he'd been gone a long time and when I went to look for him he wasn't there. And . . .'

'Yes?' Lee prompted more gently, as she clearly heard Dulcie gulp.

'I—I found a note in his room when I returned to see if he was there.'

'A note?'

'Oh, Lee,' Dulcie moaned, 'I feel terrible! I meant to put it safely away or burn it, but he must have found all the correspondence about boarding school, because he says he won't go and is running away.'

'Didn't you tell him that you'd changed your mind?'

'I should have done,' Dulcie replied, 'but we'd only talked about it before and I thought it would be easier just to forget about it. I never dreamt that he'd run away, and I've been looking everywhere. That's why I came to see you.'

Lee, feeling torn with anxiety herself, tried to explain. 'I wasn't well and I lay down after lunch and fell asleep, which was why I didn't hear you, but Trigg might have come in by the back door, which I'm sure is still open. If you hang on a minute I'll go and see if he's maybe hiding in the kitchen.'

# CHAPTER TEN

A QUICK tour of the downstairs rooms produced nothing. There was no sign of anyone. Back on the phone, though, Lee promised Dulcie, 'I'll look again, he may be hiding outside somewhere. If I find him I'll let you know immediately. Have you informed the police?'

'George has,' Dulcie choked. 'He's on his way home.'

'I'm sure he'll soon be found,' Lee said gently, for Dulcie's sake concealing her own apprehension.

'The police advised me to check any place where I think there's the slightest possibility he might be and to ask people to keep a lookout for him,' said Dulcie hollowly.

'He can't be far,' Lee tried to sound optimistic. 'Trigg may be young, but he's very sensible.'

When Dulcie rang off, she methodically searched the house again, then the outbuildings. Because both were a good size it took her a while, but she was eventually convinced that Trigg wasn't there. It was almost dark and raining hard when she decided to take a look along the river bank. She had thought of ringing Slade, having no doubt at all that he would help, but as it was unlikely that he would be back from London yet, she was reluctant to risk worrying Lydia. It was only a few miles, following the towpath, to Slade's house. By the time she walked it, if Trigg hadn't been found, Slade might have returned and would know the best thing to do.

The wind rose, driving the rain before it, and as darkness fell it became impossible to investigate all the places where a small boy might be hiding. Lee was halfway between her house and Slade's when she realised she was making little headway. Trigg could be

167

in a dozen places, and if she hadn't been so overwhelmed by anxiety she might have been aware sooner how futile it was to come here in the dark on her own.

Nevertheless, she decided to continue and consult Slade, rather than retrace her footsteps. She knew the way well, for over the years she had often wandered in this direction. Usually she had her sketching pad with her and pretended to be searching for small mammals or flora to illustrate her books, but more often she had spent most of the time just standing gazing at Slade's home, wondering what he was doing—if he would ever be back again. It seemed incredible that she could ever have gone as far as letting herself get engaged to another man. She must have used Matt in the hope that he would kill her love for Slade and enable her to lead a more normal life. It wasn't something to be proud of, and Lee's head bowed in shameful regret as she trudged on.

By the time Slade's house came in sight she was wet through and shivering, her hands, as she rang the doorbell, numb with cold. The butler answered the door, not recognising the bedraggled girl on the doorstep until she spoke.

'Miss—Lee!' his usual coolness slipping a little for once, he exclaimed in a horrified voice. 'You'd better come in. Such a terrible evening for you to be out . . .'

'Is Mr Western home yet?' Lee brushed water off her face with a nervous hand as she stepped into the opulent hall and saw how she was dripping all over the carpet.

As Higgins did his best to restrain a shudder, Slade strode from his study. 'Lee!' he took one look at the drenched state she was in and visibly whitened. 'Lee!' he repeated, his jaw clenching as he reached her side, as if he found it difficult to articulate. 'You aren't hating me this much, are you?'

What on earth was he talking about? Lee sniffed and

gulped as she pushed back her streaming hair in an attempt to see him better. For going to London, perhaps? 'Don't be silly!' she spluttered.

'I was on my way to see you,' he dismissed the curious butler. 'Don't you realise you shouldn't be running around in the rain in your condition? I suppose you received a shock, but surely it wasn't as bad as all that?'

Though she was still unable to follow him, Lee's heart warmed that he showed such concern, even if she failed to understand why he should look so pale. She ventured another guess, aloud this time. 'You've heard about Trigg?'

'Trigg?' His voice revealed that the boy had been far from his thoughts. 'No, what about him?'

Lee frowned but hurried on, 'He's disappeared—I've been out looking for him.'

It was Slade's turn to look confused. 'You haven't heard from Paul?'

Paul was his doctor friend. 'No, of course not,' she exclaimed. 'I didn't expect to. I'm worried about Trigg.'

He stared at her, appearing to be at the mercy of several conflicting emotions, all of which affected him deeply. 'We seem to be talking about different things,' he muttered thickly.

'Trigg . . .'

Slade endeavoured to pull himself together, though it was difficult when he just wanted to pull Lee close and kiss her passionately. 'Whoever's missing,' he cut in, 'you're not going to be much help to them if you go down with pneumonia. You'd better come upstairs and get out of those wet clothes.'

Feeling that was of the least importance at the moment, Lee began to protest, but he refused to listen and merely picked her up, holding her so tightly she couldn't struggle. This was the second time today she had been in his arms, and even the thought of it was enough to make her feel dizzy. He carried her to his bedroom—Lee presumed it was his owing to the size of it and its masculine decor. Putting her down in the middle of it, he began removing her coat with hands she was surprised to see were shaking.

She heard his breath catch as his glance lingered on the thrust of her breasts against the thin wet silk of her shirt, but the naked desire he betrayed, although she was shivering with cold, brought an immediate response from every nerve cell in her body. His eyes darkened and burned as her lips parted and she gazed at him helplessly. As always, she longed to throw herself into his arms. Never could two people have been closer than they had been, achieved such total completeness. She wanted him all the time until it was like a deep ache inside her.

Abruptly he turned, putting temptation behind him, but his voice was hoarse as he directed her to the en-suite bathroom. 'You'd better get out of your wet things and under the shower, Lee. Lydia is out this evening, but I'll see if I can find you something dry to put on, while you're busy.'

When he returned she had just finished and was huddled in the depth of a huge towel. He walked into the bathroom with an intimacy he seemed to take for granted but which disturbed her. He didn't even knock.

'I borrowed these from one of the maids,' he handed her a pair of jeans and a checked shirt which, although the size was about right, clashed wildly with her rich red hair. 'It's the best I could do,' he added wryly. 'You can tell me about your young friend while you're getting into them.'

He apparently had no intention of leaving her alone to dress, but because he seemed consumed by a curious anxiety, she forced herself to endure his presence. As she struggled with zips and buttons under the towel and determinedly ignored the mounting turmoil inside her, she explained about Trigg.

'He must be somewhere!' she finished apprehensively.

'The thing is, he likes the river, but it's so dangerous. That's why I walked the towpath looking for him.'

Slade went white again as he saw her stumbling blindly along it in the dark. 'It seems to me that young Trigg would be much safer at boarding school, and probably happier, once he settled down. I went and I remember I quite liked it, once I got used to it.'

But then he would have been a tough little boy! Lee glanced at him impatiently. 'So will Trigg when his health improves and he's older. He's bright and intelligent and will do well. But that's for the future. What matters now is that he's found.'

Slade nodded, giving the matter his serious attention, as Lee had known he would. 'You say he's familiar with the river?'

'Yes,' Lee replied eagerly. 'He often comes with me, or turns up while I'm there, to help me find material to illustrate my books. He appears to know what appeals to small boys better than I do.'

Slade said slowly, 'I agree with you that he's an intelligent youngster, so on a night like this, if he was looking for somewhere to hide wouldn't he be trying to find somewhere drier?'

'It's just a feeling I have about the river,' she frowned, she realised not very logically.

Slade took a tray of coffee from the maid who brought it, as they returned to the bedroom. After she had gone, he poured it out, along with a little brandy. 'Whenever a child disappears one automatically thinks of the river, if there's one near.'

'I suppose so,' sighed Lee, accepting the brandy he gave her with instruction to drink every drop. She felt warmer after the shower and with this and the coffee inside her, but no better about Trigg. 'He could be anywhere,' she admitted tearfully.

'You're fond of him, aren't you?' Slade put a comforting arm around her.

'Yes,' her lips curved tenderly. 'When the Mansfields

decided to look over The Willows, they came to River
Bend first, by mistake. Trigg wasn't much more than a
baby, and when he was taken ill they stayed for the
night as Julia was there, and a nurse. Since then he's
come to River Bend all the time. We all love him. Julia
and Sandra are going to be terribly shocked if he isn't
found.'

'He will be,' Slade promised. 'You say the police
have been informed?' When she nodded, he released
her gently and reached for the telephone. 'I'll ring
Mrs Mansfield and if he's still missing I'll see what I
can do.'

A few minutes later he replaced the receiver and
turned to Lee again. 'No luck yet. I've had a word with
his father. Naturally he's extremely worried.'

Lee could scarcely trust herself to speak. She had
been praying that Trigg had been found but had
gathered enough from Slade's conversation with George
to realise that her prayers hadn't been answered. Not
yet anyway. When Slade said he would begin looking
for Trigg immediately, she was determined to come
with him. 'If you would just run me home first,' she
begged, 'I'll get a dry coat.'

'We aren't short of waterproofs,' he retorted, 'but I'd
rather you stayed here, Lee. I don't want you taking
any more foolish risks.'

'I couldn't just sit doing nothing,' she protested
fiercely.

He continued regarding her with a worried frown,
then appeared to give in. 'It might be a good idea to go
back to River Bend and start there. It could pay to take
another look around as the boy might have been hiding
in a corner you hadn't noticed. I'll speak to the staff
before we leave, in case he turns up here.'

They were just leaving the drive when Lee remembered Slade's boat and grasped his arm so quickly
she might have caused an accident. A week ago she was
certain he would have been furious with her, and was

surprised when he merely murmured her name and pulled off the road.

'What is it!' He turned to look at her, as though he couldn't see enough of her and was ready to take advantage of any excuse to study her lovely face.

Lee swallowed in confusion at the expression in his eyes and her breathing was uneven as she answered. 'I've just remembered your boat, Slade. When your mother rang, inviting me to spend the day on the river, I had Trigg staying with me, and she invited him along as well. He loved the boat so much that we had almost to prize him off it. Do you think he could be there?'

'Most unlikely,' he replied slowly. 'It's checked every day.'

'But Trigg might not know that,' Lee argued, 'and he could have slipped aboard after whoever it is you get to check it had gone.'

Slade thought for a moment, then with a brief nod turned the car. 'We'll take a look, if only to reassure you.'

At first, Lee was sure her intuition had let her down. The boat was securely anchored, but the wind was rocking it wildly on its moorings. In such conditions it would have been difficult for anyone to board it. She was doubtful, anyway, that Trigg could have managed it—she even felt alarmed at the thought of Slade trying to. As she watched him swiftly calculating the distance to jump, she felt suddenly terrified. He had ordered her to stay where she was, but fear for him drove her to join him.

'Please don't take any risks!' she shouted above the noise of the wind. 'I probably made a mistake. I'm sure he can't be there.'

He hustled her straight back to the car, his face grim. 'If you move again,' he threatened, 'I'll lock you in! I don't take risks, and it would be a waste of time not to check, since we're here.'

Lee nodded numbly as with a brief salute he boarded

the boat and disappeared below decks. The ease with which this was completed made a mockery out of her apprehension and made her realise how extremely fit he must be. Then amazingly, within a very few minutes, he was back on deck again, carrying Trigg.

'Oh, Trigg!' She was so overcome by relief that she forgot Slade's warning and flew to meet them, flinging her arms around the boy as Slade leapt back to the landing stage and lowered him to the ground. 'What a fright you've given us! Your poor parents are frantic!'

Slade let her sit in the back of the car with him. He was shaken, but on the whole none the worse. He clung to Lee and she hugged him close. 'I was running away, Lee, because I don't want to go to boarding school,' he confessed pathetically. 'I was trying to decide where to go next when I fell asleep.'

'You aren't going to boarding school,' Lee said gently. 'Your mum and dad were only thinking about it and they decided definitely against it, days ago. Your mother meant to burn the papers you saw, but you know how she tends to forget things. But you don't have to take my word for it. Come home and they'll tell you themselves.'

For a boy so determined to leave home, it was moving to see how eager he was to return to it, yet he refused to go until Lee promised to come with him.

'I'll be there, too,' said Slade gruffly as he started the car again, 'though I'm sure you won't need either of us.'

Half an hour later they left The Willows with its family happily reunited. Trigg had flown to his mother and for several minutes they had cried over each other and kept saying they were sorry. And when George had been able to speak he had assured his son that he could complete his education at local schools and settle for just going to university—if he wanted to.

'Well, that's that,' Slade remarked broodingly, as he and Lee drove away.

'You don't sound very pleased with yourself.' Lee glanced quickly at his dark profile.

'Why should I be?' he retorted. 'You deserve all the credit.'

'We can share it, surely?' she protested. 'After all, you found him.'

'If you hadn't remembered the boat, I shouldn't have thought of it,' he rejoined abruptly.

Lee sighed. She didn't doubt that he was as pleased as she was that Trigg was safely back with his family again. It was obviously something else that was worrying him. Maybe his meeting, this afternoon, hadn't gone so well. And suddenly she recalled something else. 'You said you had something to tell me.'

'As soon as I get you inside,' he said curtly, pulling up outside River Bend. 'I still have something to ask you, as well.'

Slade wasn't given to being mysterious; when he had something to say, or wanted something, he didn't usually beat about the bush. He usually came straight out with it, so why the uncertainty she sensed now? Bitterly she decided he was about to repeat that he had no wish to see her again and to ask her arrogantly to forgive him, but when he helped her into the house as if she were something very precious, she felt more bewildered than ever.

It was still raining heavily and they got wet even in those few yards. 'I shudder to think what Trigg would have been like after spending the night on the river in weather like this!' she gasped breathlessly, as Slade closed the door behind them.

'I shudder to think what you would have been like if you'd had an accident on that towpath!' he rasped. 'I want you to promise never to do anything like that again.'

'Normally I shouldn't dream of it,' she replied absently, as he relieved her of her borrowed coat, 'but you have to admit that tonight was an emergency.'

'Even so——' he began harshly, then hesitated as he

noticed how weary she was. Her hair streamed down her back, her face was white, her eyes huge. 'You look like a lost urchin,' he sighed raggedly. 'Come on, let's go to the kitchen and I'll make some coffee.'

Lee felt terribly tired and suddenly just wanted to go to bed. The buffeting she had received from the wind and rain, along with the worry over Trigg, must have exhausted her, she decided. 'If you don't mind, I'd rather not have coffee,' she said. 'And I'm sure you would rather go straight home.'

'Are you feeling ill again?' he asked sharply, making no move to leave, his eyes fixed on her anxiously.

'No, just tired,' she replied. 'After I'd taken the medicine your friend gave me, I felt a whole lot better. It seems to have cured whatever I had,' she tried to joke.

He stared at her, his expression suddenly cold and blank enough to make her shiver. His voice was cold too as he asked, 'Haven't you really any idea what's the matter with you? What it is that's making you feel so ill?'

As she gazed back at him for interminable seconds, until comprehension finally dawned, Lee's breathing seemed to stop altogether while her eyes widened to dominate her chalky face. Oh, no, it couldn't be that! But she knew in that same instant that it was.

'I'm . . .'

'Pregnant.' Slade took pity on her inability to put it in words as he pulled her abruptly into his arms. 'I realised before that you didn't know, but I thought you did. Somehow I thought Paul had been in touch.'

Frantically she shook her head, trying to reject the horror of the truth but unable to. What fools they had been, they might have guessed what would happen! Theirs had never been a lukewarm relationship at any time, but since Slade had come back the strength of their emotions had grown explosively. How many times had the earth rocked and shattered about their heads, and now, ironically, to use a well-worn phrase, they were reaping the whirlwind!

She gulped against the extreme pain and shock racing through her. Slade was watching her, his face white, she could even feel his strong body trembling against her. And no wonder, she thought bitterly. How many times had he warned her he wouldn't be tied? If he had loved her and wanted to marry her, how happy and proud she would have been to have his child. But he didn't want her, he was so clearly wondering how he could get rid of her that she shuddered. As she gazed at him blindly, she could find no hint of anything in the hardness of the eyes that met hers to assure her otherwise. With a low cry of anguish, she wrenched herself from his arms and whirled away from him.

'You'd better go,' she cried.

'Lee!' he begged, following her as she fled across the hall, his face ashen. 'Please wait! You can't send me away like this!'

There was a note of pleading in his voice that she had never heard before, and suddenly she couldn't bear it. He was about to offer either money or pity, she was certain—maybe both. Without pausing, she raced upstairs, shouting disjointedly over her shoulder as she fled, 'I want nothing more from you! Just please close the door behind you, as you go out.'

She was shaking so badly that when she reached her room she thought she was going to collapse, and the crashing of the front door sounded like a funeral knell in her ears. Slade had left, as she had asked him to, and he wouldn't be back. Lee subsided on her bed with a tortured groan, wishing she could weep. Her heart was full of shock and tears. She felt terrible, but she was still dry-eyed in the morning.

She didn't sleep, either, and the night seemed endless. After the first shock of learning she was pregnant had worn off, she wondered why it had never occurred to her. She had had a lot on her mind lately, but it

amazed her that she hadn't given more thought to the
normal functions of her own body. Nevertheless, she
was determined to have the baby and that it shouldn't
suffer. She would devote the rest of her life to seeing it
didn't. She was probably more fortunate than many
girls in similar circumstances, as she had her own home
and could earn enough to keep both of them. Julia and
Nigel were getting married, and so, she believed, would
Matt and Sandra, in time, but she could always take in
more paying guests if necessary.

She tried but failed to stop thinking of Slade, aware
that while her thoughts clung to him they brought no
comfort. What sense was there in sentences prefaced
with If only . . .? Impatiently she told herself that the
sooner she faced reality the better. What was the use of
wishing for the moon when even the stars were out of
reach? Slade had gone and she wouldn't be seeing him
again. He could be on his way to New York by now
and making arrangements for his mother to return to
London. Lee doubted that he would allow Lydia to stay
here for fear she learned anything of what had
happened.

Hollow-eyed and weary, Lee got up as soon as dawn
arrived and took a shower. When she had finished she
slowly dried her hair, then struggled into her old
dressing gown and went downstairs. The shower hadn't
revived her much and she didn't feel hungry, but she
would try and eat something. She reminded herself that
she had two to think of now.

A watery ray of sunshine followed her over the
hall, but it wasn't until she reached the kitchen that
she realised that, apart from this geographical pheno-
menon after so much rain, she wasn't alone. Slade,
far from being in America, was slumped at the
kitchen table, his head in his hands. As Lee came in
he looked up to stare at her, his eyes burning black
coals in a face crying out for a razor. His mouth
moved, but he seemed as beyond speech as she was a

they both poised, like motionless statues, staring at each other.

Strangely enough it was Lee who recovered first. The unmistakable marks of suffering Slade bore aroused her compassion yet made her wary. She had never seen him looking less than immaculate, even in casual clothes, and his crumpled shirt, unshaven jaw and hair that looked as if a hand had been mangling it for hours was a sight she suspected few had witnessed, but what that was evidence of she couldn't be sure.

'I thought I told you to go,' she whispered. 'Didn't you hear me?'

'I'd have had to be deaf not to,' he muttered huskily, getting to his feet and joining her.

Close at hand, evidence of a sleepless night was even more apparent. He still wore the suit he had worn last night, at least part of it. The dark trousers were creased over the muscular strength of his powerful thighs and the once immaculate shirt was wrenched open at the throat, the sleeves rolled back over darkly tanned forearms. Even exhausted, Slade carried with him a force that couldn't be ignored, a masculine vitality that burned in his tired eyes like leaping flames.

'I heard the door bang,' she gulped.

'I opened and closed it again,' he retorted, 'but I couldn't leave. I wanted to follow you, even then, and make you listen, but I realised you needed time. I hoped you'd be in a more amenable mood this morning.'

'You—you haven't sat there all night?' she gasped.

Something like pain darkened his eyes. 'I tried not to fall asleep in case you needed me. I think I dozed off now and again, but you'd given me plenty to think about, and I didn't feel like sleep, anyway.'

'You look terrible!' she exclaimed, her gaze clinging to the ravages on his face, the deep-drawn lines, the whiteness under his skin.

'You don't look so good yourself,' Slade muttered dryly. 'We sound like an old married couple, don't we,

who love each other so much that tact is no longer so
necessary.'

'Only we aren't married,' Lee rejoined bleakly
wondering how he could be so callous as to taunt her
about it.

'But about to be.'

Wrapping her arms around herself in an unconsci
ously defensive gesture, Lee said raggedly, 'You're
joking, of course.'

'I'm not, little one,' his voice was suddenly thick with
tension. 'I'm asking you to marry me.'

She went white. 'You're asking me to marry you
because of the baby.' Her throat hurt, but she forced
herself to go on. 'You know it wouldn't work. Every
time you looked at me you'd feel trapped. At the fla
you said you hated me.'

He caught her close, as if determined to protect her
from any more pain. When she didn't struggle, he laid
his cheek against the top of her head and said rawly
'After that night at the flat I was determined never to
see you again, unless you agreed to comply with my
wishes and came to me of your own free will. I knew I'd
gone too far, forcing you the way I did, but while the
hurt on your face was like a sword thrusting through
my vitals, I refused to believe my heart was affected.
was convinced I didn't need a woman in my life
permanently and that I could walk away and leave you
again if necessary.'

Despising herself for being unable to move, Lee
muttered bitterly, 'What made you change your mind
It could only have been the baby.'

His arms tightened as he ignored this, but she fel
him tremble. 'I told myself when you left me in Pari
that you weren't worth the worry you put me through
No,' he corrected himself bitterly, 'I may as well be
honest—it was agony. I wanted you back so desperatel
that I didn't sleep for weeks, yet I refused to admit you
meant anything more to me than a congenia

companion. Then in New York, when I learned that you were engaged to Matt, I found an urgent business reason why it was imperative that I drop everything and return to Reading. Self-righteously, I decided I wanted no criminal in any branch of the family and that you weren't good enough for Matt or any of us.

'I was determined to break your engagement. Even when we met again and I saw you were more beautiful and enchanting than ever, even after I made love to you and all the old magic was there, stronger than ever, I still thought I could walk away.

'I was still point-blank refusing to believe I couldn't, until I met you that day in the bookshop in Reading. It was when Lydia talked of going to France for your first christening that I knew if you ever had a child I had to be its father. No other man had touched you but me, and I swore, there and then, that no one was going to. I went, the next day, and bought the ring and made the necessary arrangements for us to be married. Suddenly I couldn't wait.'

'Then why did you?' she breathed, in a daze.

'There was still a small part of me holding out,' he confessed tautly. 'Pride, I suppose. You see, I thought if you loved me you'd have tried to see me again, or at least tried to get in touch with me. As well,' his voice rasped, 'I was afraid.'

'Afraid?' It didn't seem possible!

He drew back to look down on her, his eyes tortured as they met her bewildered blue ones. 'That after the contemptible way I'd treated you, that I'd killed anything you might have felt for me? I was a coward, my darling. To live in hope seemed preferable to having my hopes smashed. It was a risk I hesitated to take.'

'Yet you asked me to go to London with you,' she whispered.

'When I found I could put off no longer,' he said thickly. 'I was going to ask you to marry me on the way and hoped—no, prayed we'd be celebrating. When I

arrived here and discovered you were feeling ill and
suspected the cause of it, it just made me love you all
the more.'

'You—you aren't just asking me because of the . . .'

'It's my baby, too, Lee,' he cut in gently, kissing her
suddenly tear-drenched cheeks adoringly. 'And I love
its mother to distraction. Surely you can't doubt that
now?'

Lee couldn't. It was written too clearly in his eyes,
along with the suffering he had endured. She hád never
seen such devotion on his face before and she felt
exultant yet strangely humble that it was for her.

'I've loved you since the beginning, I think,' she
gulped, suddenly clinging to him. 'That's why I left you
in Paris. I couldn't bear your distrust any longer. It was
bad enough before I discovered I loved you, but after
that it began making me feel ill.'

'Oh, my love,' he groaned, 'I was so wrong about
that too, if you're talking about the time I thought I
caught you stealing that necklace.' His face darkened.
'It might not have been altogether my fault for believing
you guilty of a crime you'd never committed, but I
should have known you hadn't a dishonest bone in
your whole body. Last night, when Ann Bowie came
and confessed what had really happened, I think I could
have killed her!'

Lee stiffened with shock. 'She told you . . .?'

'It must have been on her conscience,' he said grimly
'I've felt she's been trying to tell me something for a
long time.'

Knowing Ann Bowie, Lee thought that was quite
possible. Her heart warmed, then chilled. 'You won't
dismiss Ray, will you?' she asked anxiously. 'He works
for you now, doesn't he, and he's never done anything
like that again.'

'Sweetheart,' Slade muttered huskily, 'he deserves to
be punished for the false image I had of you—or felt
forced to keep of you, but after all this time it might be

etter for everyone if we just forgot about it, Besides,
'm as guilty as Ray. I let some of my father's
xperiences colour my whole life.'

'What do you mean, Slade?' she whispered compas-
onately as his face went tight. Was she about to hear
f something which she had always sensed troubled him
nd lay behind his reluctance to marry?

She listened quietly while he sighed and said tersely,
My father had brains, but he seldom used them, Lee.
Vhen he was little more than twenty, he married a
uch older woman, notorious for her scrapes with the
w. It cost my grandfather a packet to extricate him
om her last escapade. There was a divorce.
ortunately there were no children and he married
ydia, but it was years before the dust from it all
ttled. Even when I had grown up, remnants of the
candal kept resurfacing, particularly when my father,
ever a faithful husband, was killed in a car crash with
is former wife.'

So that was why Slade had always been so emphatic
aat no further hint of scandal should discredit his
amily and why he had been so wary of marriage!
Children could be extremely sensitive regarding their
arents. Slade's father might have put him off marriage
or life. Lee sighed and gently caressed the back of his
eck. 'It's all over now,' she murmured. 'Your father
aybe made mistakes, but sometimes it's better to
emember the good things about people, rather than the
ad. And, for all our sakes, it might be wiser to leave
e past where it belongs, don't you think?'

When he didn't speak, she wondered what more she
ould do to help, but apparently the love transmitted
rough her hands was enough. His eyes glowed with an
credible warmth as he bent to cover her parted lips
ith his own.

Eventually he said thickly, 'I know I'm a lot luckier
an I deserve, that you can forgive me for ever
inking you less than perfect. When I saw how you put

yourself out over that boy, the way you care for him
the trouble you go to for other people, you make m
feel very humble.'

'What about my terrible temper?' she teased, 'and
her smile innocently beguiling, 'my inclination to mak
love at all the wrong times?'

'Shameless hussy!' His eyes darkened as the
devoured her with teasing severity. 'We have things t
do today, my sweet, which for once must tak
precedence over our immediate desires—I think . . .'

A year later a private plane landed on a Greek islan
and a chauffeur-driven limousine picked up two peopl
and drove them to a white villa, perched on th
mountainside above a beautiful beach on the nort
coast of Crete. The villa, which stood in its own groun
was cool and spacious, the staff discreet. It was the firs
time the Westerns had been there since their hone
moon.

Slade said softly, as he closed their bedroom doc
before taking his wife in his arms, 'Happy anniversar
darling. I love you.'

Lee didn't doubt it, and her adoring blue eyes wer
glowing evidence that she loved him too. Any doubt
she had entertained over their marriage had long sinc
disappeared. Slade worked from home now, seldor
leaving it unless there was an emergency, and, sinc
their son had been born, unless she was with him. Th
was their first real holiday together since thei
honeymoon, and he had insisted that he must have he
to himself for a few weeks. Slade junior had been left i
the care of his nanny, with his doting grandmother an
Ann Bowie supervising. Lee hadn't been too keen o
having a nanny for her child at first, until she realise
her husband had first call on her time and that was th
way she wanted it. Slade hadn't insisted, he had left th
final decision to her, but she knew he loved her all th
more for it.

As he began kissing her, then undressing her, and his kisses deepened, she managed to whisper huskily, 'Sofia said dinner was almost ready.'

'Who's interested in dinner?' he muttered hoarsely, picking her up and carrying her to the bed. Seconds later they were drifting in an even more magic world than the one outside. Slade was a skilful lover with a totally responsive wife, but the incredible excitement of their coming together was always new. Slade's clothes joined hers on the floor, a button tearing as undisguised desire flared in his dark eyes, and as he gathered Lee to him, she felt him trembling against her.

Soon they were a tangle of straining arms and limbs, with inflamed senses already crying out for release. Lee was struck, as always, by the terrifying power of their attraction. As soon as they touched their flesh would burn in the current that passed between them. He kissed her face, her neck, her breasts and thighs, letting his mouth linger as he called her name. His hands and mouth incited her almost beyond endurance, then, when she thought she could bear it no longer, he joined them in an explosion of feeling so powerful that she cried out. Together they soared in an eruption of ecstasy and pleasure to that other realm they were now very familiar with but which, as always, seemed just the beginning.

A loud knocking on the door and a grumbling warning from Sofia, who had known Slade all his life, that dinner would be ruined if they didn't hurry, brought them reluctantly back to earth again.

'Ah, well,' sighed Lee in the middle of it, 'if we spend much more time here, it won't be long before our son has company in his nursery.'

'He's going to anyway,' teased Slade, his eyes on the lush slenderness of his young wife rather than the clock. 'At least half a dozen brothers and sisters, wouldn't you say?'

He got a pillow thrown at him for his pains as Lee

hurriedly left the bed in an attempt to appease Sofia, but her heart was singing. Whatever Slade wanted, she would try and give him. She was wise enough to realise they shared a relationship to be treasured. Once she had thought never to see Slade again. Now he had been her husband for a year and a loving father for four months. What more could she ask?

'Nothing!' she exclaimed aloud, on a high happy note as Sofia sounded a last dire warning, thinking, Lee suspected, as Slade turned on his broad back and laughed, that the English were all slightly crazy!

'What was that all about, my love?' He made a pretence of being anxious. 'I hope Sofia doesn't think you were telling her we don't want any dinner.'

Lee's eyes widened in dismay. 'She wouldn't think that, would she?'

'She might,' he grinned, catching the unwary hand she lowered to topple her down beside him. 'Would it matter?'

Tumbled against him, she couldn't resist putting her arms around him again. 'No,' she murmured, cheeks pink, 'it wouldn't.'

'On the other hand,' he teased, 'it looks as if I'm going to need all the strength I can find if I'm to keep this up, so maybe we should go and eat?'

Much later, as they took a midnight stroll along the seashore before turning in, Slade took her in his arms and said, 'Do you know, this last year has been the happiest in my life, my darling.'

'For me, too.' Lee lifted her own arms and wrapped them around his neck. Secure in the knowledge of his love, tears glinted suddenly in her eyes. 'You've given me so much,' she whispered unevenly. 'I wish there was some new and splendid way of saying I love you.'

The kiss he gave her in return was incredibly gentle, a communication that went beyond words. 'Just keep on caring for me,' he said huskily, 'exactly as you're doing now. And as long as we have each other, that's all that matters.'

And, as his lips closed once more over hers, Lee could only show him silently how much she agreed.

# Coming Next Month in Harlequin Presents!

**847  LION OF DARKNESS   Melinda Cross**
The New York doctor, who's helped so many cope with blindness in
a sighted world, is baffled by his latest case—and a force that
threatens the doctor–patient relationship.

**848  THE ARROGANT LOVER   Flora Kidd**
A young widow distrusts the man who tries to come between her
and her Scottish inheritance. He made love to her, then left
without a word nine years ago. Why should she trust him now?

**849  GIVE ME THIS NIGHT   Vanessa James**
Passion flares between a tour guide and a mystery writer on the
Greek island of Paxos. But she's blundered into his life at the worst
possible moment—because around him, she senses danger!

**850  EXORCISM   Penny Jordan**
Once she naively assumed he'd marry her if they made love. Now
he wants her to help him research his new book in the Caribbean.
Why? To exorcise the past?

**851  SLEEPING DESIRE   Charlotte Lamb**
After a year apart, can an estranged wife forget the solicitor's
letters and the divorce proceedings? Easily—when the man she
loves reawakens her desire.

**852  THE DEVIL'S PRICE   Carole Mortimer**
The day she left him, their love turned to ashes. But a London
singer is willing to bargain with the devil to be with her lover
again—but not as his wife!

**853  SOUTH SEAS AFFAIR   Kay Thorpe**
Against her better judgment, against all her values, a young
woman allows herself to be drawn into a passionate affair with
her father's archenemy!

**854  SUN LORD'S WOMAN   Violet Winspear**
Fate, which seemed to have been so kind, deals a cruel blow to a
young woman on her wedding night, and her husband's desert
kingdom loses its dreamlike appeal.

Author **JOCELYN HALEY**,
also known by her fans as **SANDRA FIELD**
and **JAN MACLEAN**, now presents her
eighteenth compelling novel.

# DREAM OF DARKNESS

With the help of the enigmatic Bryce Sanderson,
Kate MacIntyre begins her search for the meaning behind
the nightmare that has haunted her since childhood.
Together they will unlock the past and forge a future.

**Available at your favorite
retail outlet in NOVEMBER.**

# WORLDWIDE LIBRARY IS YOUR TICKET TO ROMANCE, ADVENTURE AND EXCITEMENT

## Experience it all in these big, bold Bestsellers— Yours exclusively from WORLDWIDE LIBRARY WHILE QUANTITIES LAST